PUBLIC ADMINISTRATION TRAINING CENTER
University of Minnesota

STUDIES IN ADMINISTRATION · NUMBER ONE

THE MINNESOTA COMMISSION OF ADMINISTRATION AND FINANCE

1925–1939

An Administrative History

COMMITTEE ON TRAINING FOR PUBLIC ADMINISTRATION, UNIVERSITY OF MINNESOTA

Members of the Committee, 1941–42

WILLIAM ANDERSON, Chairman, *Professor and Chairman of the Department of Political Science*

GAYLORD W. ANDERSON, *Professor and Head of the Department of Preventive Medicine and Public Health*

FREDERIC H. BASS, *Professor of Municipal and Sanitary Engineering and Head of the Department of Civil Engineering*

THEODORE C. BLEGEN, *Dean of the Graduate School and Professor of History*

F. STUART CHAPIN, *Professor and Chairman of the Department of Sociology and Director of the Graduate Course in Social Work*

EDWARD M. FREEMAN, *Dean of the College of Agriculture, Forestry, and Home Economics*

CLARENCE C. LUDWIG, *Associate Professor of Political Science, Chief of the Municipal Reference Bureau, and Executive Secretary of the League of Minnesota Municipalities*

HORACE E. READ, *Professor of Law*

RUSSELL A. STEVENSON, *Dean of the School of Business Administration*

JOHN T. TATE, *Dean of the College of Science, Literature, and the Arts, and Professor of Physics*

LLOYD M. SHORT, Secretary, *Professor of Political Science*

Public Administration Training Center Staff

LLOYD M. SHORT, *Director*

EUNICE E. CHAPIN, *Secretary*
MYRTLE J. EKLUND, *Librarian*

WILLIAM H. ANDERSON,
Research Assistant

The Minnesota Commission of Administration and Finance

1925–1939

AN ADMINISTRATIVE HISTORY

BY

LLOYD M. SHORT, Ph.D.

Professor of Political Science and Director of the
Public Administration Training Center at the
University of Minnesota

AND

CARL W. TILLER, A.M.

Executive Assistant to the Director, Municipal Finance Officers
Association, and Sometime In-Service Fellow in Public Administration, University of Minnesota

THE UNIVERSITY OF MINNESOTA PRESS
Minneapolis

PRINTED AT THE LUND PRESS, INC., MINNEAPOLIS

1 0

To

MORRIS B. LAMBIE

Professor of Political Science and Chief of the Municipal Reference Bureau in the University of Minnesota and Executive Secretary of the League of Minnesota Municipalities from 1922 to 1935, whose knowledge, vision, enthusiasm, and good will contributed so much to the progress of municipal and state administration in Minnesota and to the establishment of graduate training in public administration at the University of Minnesota.

PREFACE

THE movement for administrative reorganization — including the consolidation of departments, the extension of the governor's authority to direct and supervise administration, and the establishment of auxiliary services with substantial powers of control over line departments and agencies — was unquestionably the most significant trend in American state government during the early part of the twentieth century. Beginning about 1910, state after state conducted investigations and adopted statutes or constitutional amendments aimed at making their administrative systems more nearly adequate to the added demands put upon them by the constant increase in the number and scope of governmental functions and activities.

Minnesota was one of the first states to give attention to this problem. An Efficiency and Economy Commission appointed by Governor Eberhart in 1913 submitted a significant report in 1914 calling for departmental reorganization, an executive budget system, and the merit system in state civil service. A budget plan was adopted in 1915, and, following the report of a legislative interim committee in 1917, certain minor departmental changes were made and limited central purchasing was introduced. However, it was not until the passage of the administrative reorganization act of 1925, following the submission of a report by an interim committee of the House of Representatives, that Minnesota joined the growing number of states which had achieved a major administrative reform.

Because of the significance of the state administrative reorganization movement, the attempt to formulate principles of administrative organization and procedure that would serve as a guide to future programs of action, and the extravagant claims which were sometimes made for the benefits that had been or could be derived from such measures, students of public administration have undertaken with varying degrees of success to appraise the movement. One of the greatest obstacles to such appraisals has been the lack of detailed and accurate data concerning the actual operation of state agencies established or altered by the reorganization programs. Practicing administrators have lacked time or motivation to undertake the task, and students of administration, unable to gain the necessary approval and cooperation to make such investigations, have had to be content with tracing the legislative history of reorganization measures and making rather cursory observations of results based upon published reports and documents. Comparative studies have been almost impossible.

The passage of a second major reorganization statute in Minnesota in 1939, resulting in the replacement of the three-member Commission of Administration and Finance established in 1925 by a single-headed Department of Administration, seemed to offer an unusual opportunity for making a detailed and critical study of the commission, which not only might contribute an interesting and informative history of a significant state administrative institution, but would also serve as a case study of attempted state integration through an agency responsible to the governor. Furthermore, the experience of the commission in the performance of such auxiliary or institutional services as budgeting, personnel, purchasing, and postauditing promised to throw additional light upon the difficult problems arising in the relationship between such an agency and the operating departments where the former is vested with important powers of control over the latter.

The fact that most of the persons who had been closely associated with the commission and its work in either an official or an unofficial capacity were still living, and that the necessary documentary material was available either in the files of the new Department of Administration or at the Minnesota Historical Society also suggested the feasibility of such a study.

It is evident that such an undertaking would have come to naught without the generous assistance and cooperation of many individuals. Theodore C. Christianson, who served as governor of Minnesota during the formative years of the commission, and several former members and employees of the commission were exceedingly helpful in interpreting for us significant events, policies, and actions. We are indebted especially to Mrs. Jean Wittich, budget commissioner from 1931 to 1933, for permitting us to draw upon her excellently arranged and documented personal scrapbook. Mr. A. R. Rathert, personnel assistant in the office of the commission in 1933–34, contributed many helpful suggestions. The staff of the Minnesota Historical Society and Miss Myrtle Eklund, librarian of the Public Administration Training Center Library, were very kind in locating desired papers, documents, and other materials. The state Department of Administration gave us permission to examine the files covering the period of the commission's history. Our specific obligations to earlier students of related aspects of Minnesota government are indicated in footnote references.

Mr. Ernest A. Engelbert, research assistant in the Public Administration Training Center in 1939–40, collected and organized much of the required material and directed two NYA assistants in the gathering of data from the newspaper files in the Minnesota Historical Society. Mr. John C. Jordan, research assistant during the summer of 1941, checked the footnote references, and Miss Eunice Chapin, secretary in the training center, aided in many of the details incident to the preparation and revision of the manuscript. Miss Mildred Hardin, a university student, labored diligently through many uncomfortable summer days in taking dictation and in typing and retyping the original manuscript. Miss Jean Steiner contributed many helpful suggestions in editing the manuscript for the University Press. Mr. William H. Anderson, research assistant in 1941–42, prepared the index.

The authors are deeply indebted to Professor William Anderson of the University of Minnesota, Professor Oliver P. Field of Indiana University, and Professor Morris B. Lambie of Harvard University, for reading the entire manuscript and through their comments and suggestions giving us the benefit of their intimate knowledge of Minnesota state government and administration and of the personalities and events associated with the creation and operation of the Commission of Administration and Finance.

Finally, the senior author wishes to recognize his obligation to his associate, Mr. Carl W. Tiller, whose intimate acquaintance with the work of the commission, gained through several years of service in the important position of budget secretary, contributed greatly to whatever merit the study may possess.

The prosecution of this study and its publication have been made possible by the gift of the Rockefeller Foundation to the University of Minnesota in support of the graduate training program in public administration established in 1936–37, and the project was approved by the university Committee on Training for Public Administration.

The recognition here given to those who have assisted in the preparation and publication of this volume is not intended to absolve the authors of any errors of omission or commission they may have made. The authors are aware of at least some of its shortcomings, especially those resulting from their inability to make a thorough investigation

COMMISSION OF ADMINISTRATION AND FINANCE

of the experiences and viewpoints of the operating departments, agencies, and institutions in their numerous relationships with the commission, but if they have contributed in some measure to our knowledge of this important aspect of public administration and have provided the people of Minnesota with a readable and substantially accurate account of the history of one of their most significant governmental institutions, they will feel amply rewarded.

L. M. S. and C. W. T.

Minneapolis, February 1942

TABLE OF CONTENTS

COMMISSION OF ADMINISTRATION AND FINANCE

TABLE OF CONTENTS

xiii

Chapter 1

ESTABLISHMENT OF THE DEPARTMENT OF ADMINISTRATION AND FINANCE

THE Minnesota Department of Administration and Finance can best be understood in the light of the forces and events leading up to its creation. In this chapter are traced the important steps toward administrative and financial reorganization in Minnesota state government during the first two and a half decades of the twentieth century, the work of the committee that prepared the reorganization plan of 1925, and the passage of the reorganization act.

Five important influences upon the entire fourteen-year history of the Commission of Administration and Finance are rooted in the events leading up to the establishment of the commission: (1) opposition of a group of Senate leaders, which was to have its effect not only upon the form of the 1925 legislation but also upon its subsequent functioning, (2) choice of a three-man commission rather than a single-headed department, (3) creation of a personnel division but with no provision for a merit system, (4) lack of complete centralization in matters of purchasing and personnel, due to the preserving of the independence of the Board of Control and the state institutions in these matters, and (5) emphasis on economy and control of expenditures rather than on the possibilities of the new administrative department as a staff and coordinating agency of the governor.

Beginnings of Central Control

From the organization of the state government in 1858 down to the close of the nineteenth century, Minnesota was a pioneer state with a rapidly expanding population and with a corresponding increase in agricultural activities, commerce, and industry. During this entire period the state government was constantly growing and developing to keep pace with the needs of the people. As new needs arose, successive legislatures created new state boards, commissions, departments, and institutions to care for them. Very

1

little thought was given to the coordination of the state administration.[1]

One of the first attempts to bring some semblance of centralized control and coordination into state administration occurred in 1899, when Governor John Lind submitted to the state legislature a plan for a Board of Control. He suggested that one board be created to take over the management of the state penal and charitable institutions, which up to this time had been managed by separate boards. The suggestion was ignored.

Governor Samuel R. Van Sant in his 1901 inaugural urged upon the legislature the same plan of creating a Board of Control, patterned after the single, salaried boards that had been established in Wisconsin and Iowa. The House of Representatives acceded to the governor's request and passed a bill providing for such a board to take over the management of the penal and charitable institutions. When the bill reached the Senate that body added the financial management of the university, the state normal schools, the state public school, and the schools for the deaf and the blind to the duties of the new board.[2] The House agreed to the Senate amendments, the measure was promptly signed by the governor, and the first state Board of Control was appointed in 1901.[3]

In his message to the 1903 legislature the governor urged restoration of the university and the normal schools to independent status, but the legislators were not ready to tamper with the new setup. The request was renewed in 1905, however, and this time the legislature agreed that the educational institutions should not be classed with the penal and charitable institutions of the state. A law was enacted to relieve the Board of Control of its duties relating to the university and the normal schools, except in matters of fuel supply and the construction and insurance of buildings.[4]

[1] Various studies of state administrative development in Minnesota offer the following approximate figures as to the number of state agencies in existence at stated intervals: 1860, 13; 1900, 51; 1912, 62; 1924, 92. Cf. *Preliminary Report of the Minnesota Efficiency and Economy Commission*, 1914, p. 17; *Fourth Biennial Report of the Minnesota Tax Commission*, 1914, pp. 158–75; Morris B. Lambie, *Administration of the State of Minnesota* (League of Minnesota Municipalities Bulletin No. 3, Minneapolis, 1924), pp. 6–7.

[2] Whether the amendments were made in good faith or in an attempt to kill the bill — as some students believe — is a matter of speculation.

[3] *Session Laws*, 1901, Ch. 122.

[4] *Ibid.*, 1905, Ch. 119. The entire management of the state public school (a receiving home for dependent children) and the schools for the deaf and the blind was transferred to the Board of Control in 1917 (*ibid.*, 1917, Chs. 309, 490).

ESTABLISHMENT OF THE DEPARTMENT

The next serious consideration of governmental reorganization came in 1911, probably stimulated by President Taft's Efficiency and Economy Commission, whose studies revealed a need for changes in the national administrative structure. To the 1911 legislature Governor A. O. Eberhart made an exhaustive statement concerning the state's administrative system, pointing out the lack of adequate centralization, lines of responsibility, and coordination, and pleading for legislative cooperation in effecting a reorganization. A resolution providing for an interim investigation along this line passed the House but failed in the Senate. In 1913 a resolution providing for an interim committee on state reorganization again passed the House of Representatives, but once more it was effectively blocked in the Senate.[5]

The Efficiency and Economy Commission

After adjournment of the 1913 session of the legislature Governor Eberhart appointed an Efficiency and Economy Commission of thirty public-spirited citizens. It had no appropriation from the state, its members served without pay or expense allowance, and it raised by private subscription the funds necessary for the employment of an executive secretary, for printing its reports, and for other general expenses. The commission began its work in November 1913, divided itself into committees, studied thoroughly the whole subject of Minnesota state administration, made a preliminary report on May 25, 1914, and presented a final report in the form of a suggested civil administration code in November 1914.[6]

The plan presented by the commission embraced three main features: (1) the reorganization of the state civil administration, (2) the merit system in the civil service, and (3) the budget system in state finances. The preliminary report called for the grouping of many of the state services under six main departments. Four were to be headed by single executives appointed by the governor; the fifth, the Department of Finance, to be headed by an elective state official, the treasurer; and the sixth, the Department of Edu-

---

[5] It is of interest to note that Henry Rines, who later became the first chairman of the Commission of Administration and Finance, was speaker of the House in 1913. A. J. Peterson, Minnesota's first budget commissioner, was a member of the House that year.

[6] Dr. E. Dana Durand of the University of Minnesota, former director of the United States Census Bureau, served as consulting statistician to the commission.

cation, to be under board control.[7] The commission had decided to present its preliminary report early for a double purpose — to create public interest in the subject and to give the commission a chance to test and revise its recommendations in the light of public discussion and debate.

Although the preliminary report had provoked considerable discussion and some attacks upon the far-reaching changes that its adoption would produce, the commission in its final report conformed to the original plan with one exception: The proposed Department of Finance was entirely omitted.[8] The other five principal departments, the proposed establishment of a merit system for state personnel under a civil service board, and the plan for a budget system under direction of the governor were all retained in the final report.[9]

The 1915 legislature had before it a number of bills dealing with items contained in the commission report,[10] Governor Hammond commended the report in his inaugural and in a special message, and the newspapers expressed general approval. However, when the session ended, the only results [11] were the passage of the commission's bill providing for a biennial budget to be prepared by the governor and the creation of a legislative interim committee to give further study to civil administration and to report back

[7] *Preliminary Report of the Efficiency and Economy Commission*, 1914. On the subject of civil service the commission wrote: "To prevent any possible abuse of the power lodged in the governor and the directors, the merit system in civil service is necessary" (*ibid.*, p. 9).

[8] The original report had provided for the Department of Finance (under direction of the state treasurer) to take over numerous staff functions, including the purchase of departmental supplies, the supervision of state printing, and the care of the capitol building, as well as the collection of revenues and the custody and disbursement of funds. Accounting and auditing, both pre-audit and postaudit, were to be under supervision of the state auditor, an elective official outside of the six main departments.

[9] *Final Report of the Efficiency and Economy Commission*, 1914. The departments proposed by the commission were Public Domain, Public Welfare, Education, Labor and Commerce, and Agriculture.

[10] Progress of the bills in the 1915 legislature is traced in Gilbert W. Cooke, "The Evolution of the Minnesota Budget System," an unpublished thesis in the University of Minnesota Library, 1925. Progress of the reorganization bill in the 1925 legislature also is related in the thesis.

[11] Two minor reorganization bills also passed. One, substituting a full-time game and fish commissioner for an unpaid commission, became law; the other, transferring duties of the hotel inspector to the Department of Dairy and Food, was vetoed by the governor. The 1915 legislature also proposed to the electorate a constitutional amendment authorizing the governor to reduce items in appropriation bills, in addition to the power he already possessed to veto items entirely. This proposal does not appear in the recommendations of the Efficiency and Economy Commission. At the 1916 election the proposed amendment received a vote of 136,700 for and 83,324 against, but it failed to get the required majority of the 416,215 votes cast that year.

4

in 1917.[12] Reasons for the rough treatment given by the legislature
to the Efficiency and Economy Commission's report are not hard
to find: [13] (1) jealousy because the report was the work of an
extralegal citizen body, rather than of legislators; (2) antipathy
because the recommendations ran counter to a long and deep-
seated tradition that boards and commissions were superior to
single commissioners; (3) unwillingness of a Republican majority in
the legislature to give more power to a Democratic governer; [14] (4)
neither the politicians nor the public in general were ready for a
civil service merit system; and (5) the legislators saw very little
advantage for themselves in the passage of such legislation.[15]

Operation of the 1915 Budget Act

The budget act of 1915 conformed very closely, even in its
wording, to the recommendations made by the Efficiency and
Economy Commission. By its terms state departments and agencies
were directed to file with the governor the estimates of their appropriation needs and certain other specified information (on uniform budget blanks) by December 1 preceding a regular legislative
session. The governor was authorized "in consultation with the
chief executive officers, to make final revision of the estimates,
having in view the total expenditures, the total revenues and the
[resulting] tax levy," [16] and to submit the budget to the legislature
by February 1. The law also provided that appropriations be
divided into allotments by the spending authorities, such allotments and changes in them to be filed with the state auditor. It

[12] *Session Laws*, 1915, Ch. 356.
[13] J. S. Young, former University of Minnesota professor, suggests another reason:
strong lobbying against the proposals by state officers and employees whose positions
or powers would have been affected. See his articles entitled "Reorganization of the
Administrative Branch of the Minnesota Government," in *Minnesota Law Review*,
10:40–47 (December 1925), and in *American Political Science Review*, 20:69–76 (February 1926).
[14] Winfield S. Hammond, Democrat, had been elected in 1914, but the majority in
the legislature, which had been elected without party designation, were actually
Republican.
[15] The budget bill would help the legislative appropriation and finance committees
in that it not only would give them a table of budget requests, including totals, at the
beginning of each session, but would also make sure that departments would have
determined their requests and be ready to present them orally by the time the session
started. The reorganization and civil service proposals contained no particular promises
that they would be of distinct advantage to the legislature. Significantly the budget
bill was passed; the others were not.
[16] *Session Laws*, 1915, Ch. 356, Sec. 5. The "chief executive officers" apparently
referred to the other elective officials designated in the constitution (Art. V, Sec. 1).

required that accounts of allotments and expenditures chargeable to them be kept either by the auditor himself or by the departments, subject to the auditor's inspection.

The allotment and accounting provisions of the act were never used. The provisions with reference to the preparation and submission of the biennial budget were followed at first, but during the next ten years practice with respect to the biennial budget departed farther and farther from the actual intent of the 1915 law.

The first budget estimates to be submitted under the new law came to the attention of Governor J. A. A. Burnquist in December 1916. After a conference with the "chief executive officers" on December 29, he prepared and submitted to the 1917 legislature two companion documents. One was a brief pamphlet setting forth the appropriations made by the 1915 legislature and the departmental requests for appropriations for the ensuing biennium; the other, a message and table indicating the various specific revisions and reductions that he proposed in the departmental estimates.[17] He also asked that the date for submission of estimates be moved up to August 15, so that he could hold hearings on the requests; and he requested the employment of additional help in preparing the budget.

Two years later Governor Burnquist submitted a somewhat similar budget document containing the requests of the departments and spaces for noting legislative action, but instead of submitting a second document of detailed recommendations for revisions in the departmental estimates, he sent along a two-page message, stating that the governor agreed with the departmental requests and had no changes to suggest.[18] Thereafter the budget estimates were sent to the legislature without the governor's recommendations for specific changes or revisions. By 1923 Governor J. A. O. Preus had arrived at an interpretation of the budget law which held that the governor was not required to submit an

[17] *Estimates of Appropriations Required for the biennial period ending July 31, 1919*, and *Governor's Message and Revision of Estimates of Appropriations Required for the biennial period ending July 31, 1919*.

[18] *Estimates of Appropriations Required for the biennial period ending July 31, 1921*, and *Message from the Governor, January 31, 1919*. Two factors were probably responsible for the governor's failure to prepare recommended budget revisions in 1918: Rapidly rising price trends made departmental requests for increased appropriations somewhat justifiable, and additional responsibilities incident to the World War and his duties on the Minnesota Public Safety Commission gave the governor little time for budget matters.

executive-type budget.[19] Preus did undertake to have printed in full the detailed budget requests and explanations of the departments.[20]

During the entire time that the 1915 budget law was in effect the governors recommended that it be strengthened, particularly with respect to providing the governor with a "budget officer" or "budget secretary." Burnquist, after both the 1917 and the 1919 regular sessions of the legislature ignored his request for a budget officer, even included this recommendation in his opening message to the 1919 special session, which was called to vote on the woman suffrage amendment to the United States constitution.[21] Preus, too, recommended legislation establishing a "real budget system."[22] Three times Representative Theodore Christianson, chairman of the House Appropriations Committee, introduced a bill to strengthen the budget system, three times it passed the House, and on each occasion it was killed in the Senate.

The Reorganization Movement, 1915–25

The 1915 legislature, which had ignored most of the citizens' committee recommendations, created its own Interim Committee

[19] "You will observe that I have not made definite recommendations as to what should be done in many cases. This is not required under Chapter 356, Laws of 1915. The statute reads, 'It shall be the duty of the Governor, not later than December 31 immediately preceding each regular session of the legislature, to assemble all estimates so prepared and in consultation with the chief executive officers to make final revisions of such estimates. . . .' I have not construed this language to mean that the Governor, who must necessarily approve or disapprove all appropriations made by the legislature, should, before the legislature gives consideration to appropriations, go on record in all cases as to what his future action may be. Neither the appropriation power nor responsibility should be usurped by the executive. It should be left with the legislature" (*Budget Message of J. A. O. Preus,* January 8, 1923, p. 36).

[20] This detailed budget was a separate document from the brief summary of requests (usually about 25 pages) that contained spaces for noting legislative action, which also was prepared in Preus's administration along the same lines as the one prepared in 1919 by Governor Burnquist. The detailed budget ran 300 pages in 1923 and 171 in 1925, the difference being due to the omission of the Board of Control's estimates for the institutions in the latter document. The Board of Control did not at any time abandon its practice, established in its early years, of preparing and printing its own budget booklet, in which it attempted to justify the requested appropriations for the state institutions under its supervision.

[21] "In order that Minnesota may have an up-to-date budget system, the Governor should be given the help necessary for the careful preparation of a budget. This can be done most simply and expeditiously by providing a budget officer who shall devote all his time to the study of the finances of the State. . . . If such an officer is not provided for, the Governor should be relieved of the preparation of the budget" (*Message of Governor J. A. A. Burnquist to the Special Session of the Legislature, 1919*).

[22] See his budget messages, referred to above. In 1923 he said, "I wish to renew the recommendations made two years ago that legislation be passed giving the state a real budget system." In 1925 he submitted the budget to the incoming governor with the

on Civil Administration. After this committee reported in 1917, laws were enacted making some changes in connection with education and a few other departments but no major reorganization resulted. The legislature was impressed with the desirability of centralized purchasing, however, and so it also enacted a law directing the four-member Board of Control to add purchasing for all state departments to its duties relating to state institutions and public welfare.[23] The only change in practice resulting from this law was that the board opened a "central store" to handle office supplies for state departments.

During the period from 1917 to 1923 the people were concerned primarily with the war situation and with postwar economic adjustments; problems of civil administration and governmental reorganization did not capture the public interest. In 1921 Representative Theodore Christianson introduced in the House a resolution calling for a joint Interim Committee to study problems of state administrative organization.[24] The House passed this resolution, but it was killed in the Senate Finance Committee.[25] In 1923 a similar proposal was advanced, but when it became apparent that again the Senate would not pass it, a new resolution was introduced that called for an Interim Committee of the House of Representatives alone rather than a joint committee representing both House and Senate. The House adopted this resolution unanimously on April 19, 1923. The speaker, W. I. Nolan, who had been named committee chairman by the resolution, appointed W. I. Norton, Theodore Christianson, J. B. Gislason, and Henry Spindler to complete the committee's membership.

statement: "Let me express my sincere hope that you will succeed in your efforts to have a real budget law enacted."

[23] "It shall be the duty of the State Board of Control to purchase for all the governmental departments of the State of Minnesota, not now under the financial or exclusive management of said board, all stationery, furniture, supplies, and equipment now or hereafter required by law to be furnished by the state, and for such purposes the board may appoint a purchasing agent and fix his compensation, who under its direction and subject to its rules shall attend to such purchases" (*Session Laws*, 1917, Ch. 174, Sec. 1).

[24] Christianson was identified with reorganization from his first term as a representative in 1915, when he was the only member to serve on both House committees that were considering the 1913 Efficiency and Economy Commission's report: the regular Civil Administration Committee and the special committee appointed by the speaker. Christianson's position as chairman of the House Appropriations Committee in 1919, 1921, and 1923 gave him firsthand knowledge of the complexities of the state administrative structure.

[25] The resolution, instead of going to the Civil Administration Committee or the Rules Committee, was sent to the Finance Committee, where it was pigeonholed.

The resolution provided that the committee's duties were "to investigate into the feasibility and advisability of consolidation of all co-relating departments, eliminating superfluous bureaus and departments, and reduction of the number of employees wherever necessary." The committee was given full power to subpoena witnesses, to compel their attendance, to compel the production of records and documents, and to employ necessary help and assistance.

The committee went to work in earnest. It first submitted a questionnaire to every department and agency in the state asking information on organization, functions, field of activities, personnel, income, expenses, and financial management. At a series of hearings the committee examined the heads of departments and others. Communications with other states brought information concerning their reorganization and their studies of civil administration. Finally, after the 1924 election two of the committee members, Christianson and Nolan, visited several other states that had recently reorganized their governments, including Illinois and Massachusetts.

Strong support for, and leadership of, the reorganization movement came from the Minnesota League of Women Voters. The league conducted institutes and schools all over the state to hear discussions of the need for reorganization.[26] From their work came a Citizens' Committee, on which women voters and other groups were represented and which took over direction of the movement.[27] Representatives of the league kept in close touch with the Interim Committee and later with House and Senate leaders during the hearings and debate on the reorganization bill. Altogether, it was a convincing demonstration of what an alert, well-organized, and intelligently led group of citizens can do in influencing governmental action.

The League of Minnesota Municipalities also supported the movement with resolutions passed at both its 1922 and 1923 annual meetings and with the publication in 1924 of a seventy-one-page study by Professor Morris Lambie, its executive secretary, present-

[26] Mrs. Jean Wittich, as chairman of the league's Department of Efficiency in Government, was prominent in this work; she was later to be a member of the Commission of Administration and Finance.

[27] Edna H. Akre, "The League of Women Voters: Its Organization and Work," an unpublished thesis in the University of Minnesota Library, 1926, pp. 40–41.

9

ing the problems of administrative organization and describing the structure and activities of existing state departments and agencies.[28] The Minnesota Tax Conference, meeting in January 1924, expressed confidence in the Interim Committee and pledged its support to the accomplishment of the objects toward which the committee was working.[29]

In the 1924 election two members of the House Interim Committee, Christianson and Nolan, decided to run for governor and lieutenant governor, respectively; both were nominated in the Republican primary. Christianson conducted his whole campaign upon the twin issues of governmental reorganization and economy. It was a propitious moment for such a campaign: In the national field Calvin Coolidge was being returned to the White House on a reputation for economy; and in the state the voters were concerned over the 100 per cent increase in appropriations from 1915 to 1923 and the fifteen million dollars outstanding in certificates of indebtedness. Farmers and real-estate owners were demanding reduction in property-tax levies. Christianson and Nolan were successful in their campaigns for governor and lieutenant governor.

Report of the Interim Committee, 1925

The inaugural address of Governor Christianson paved the way for the report of the Interim Committee. He called attention to the need for reorganization, outlined in a general way the essential recommendations of the Interim Committee, and enunciated a set of principles to guide the legislature in holding down appropriations. The governor supplemented and enlarged upon this phase of his inaugural address in other public speeches to various organizations and meetings during the month of January.[30]

On January 28 the Interim Committee presented its report to the House of Representatives.[31] The committee's findings were:

[28] *Administration of the State of Minnesota.* (See footnote 1, page 2). Professor Lambie also was in close personal contact with members of the Interim Committee and his familiarity with the Massachusetts Commission on Administration and Finance undoubtedly influenced the committee's decision in favor of the Massachusetts plan.

[29] *Minnesota Municipalities,* 9:18 (February 1924).

[30] The governor especially emphasized the need for a system of expenditure control to accompany administrative consolidation. He pointed out the obvious limitations of legislative control and concluded: "The only way to compel the administrative departments to exercise the most rigid economy is to lodge in the Executive the power to limit expenditures" (*Inaugural Message of Governor Theodore Christianson to the Legislature of Minnesota,* January 7, 1925, pp. 5–6).

[31] Printed in the *House Journal,* January 28, 1925, and also printed in a separate booklet under the title *Reorganization of State Government, Report of Interim Committee to House of Representatives,* 1925.

ESTABLISHMENT OF THE DEPARTMENT

1. That the lack of any effective centralized control of state expenditures permits of and breeds waste and extravagance. At present there are 92 independent spending agencies, free from any control or check except such as may be exercised by the Legislature in making appropriations, by the State Auditor in passing upon the legality of expenditures, and by the Public Examiner in making examinations of the various departments. Clearly the control exercised by the Legislature is inadequate. . . . After appropriations are made and the Legislature adjourns, its supervision ceases and no central authority has the power to pass upon the wisdom or propriety of the expenditures of the various departments or check or limit the same.

2. That the present budget law is inadequate in that it does not provide the Governor with proper facilities for the collection of the necessary data for the preparation of a scientific budget based on the actual needs of the various departments. Under existing law, the budget can be little more than a compilation of requests of the departments with such minor changes as the Governor, without facilities for a scientific preparation of a budget, may make before submitting the same to the Legislature.

3. That no provision for an effective pre-audit exists.

4. That there is a lack of any proper classification or standardization of employments or of salaries, wages, hours or titles of employees, a lack of reciprocity between departments in the use of employees and no merit system provided for by law for the selection thereof. . . .

5. That the inspectional activities of the State are not sufficiently centralized or correlated.

6. That needless departments exist and in some instances similar or related functions are placed in separate departments resulting in duplications of effort and activity and a loss both in efficiency and economy.[32]

To remedy these defects the committee proposed reorganization of the administrative branch of state government into twelve main departments and a small number of minor agencies. The committee recommended that nine of the proposed departments should follow the traditional board type of departmental organization,[33] while three should be under single commissioners.[34] Keystone of the struc-

[32] *Ibid.*, pp. 10–11.

[33] Contemporary evidence indicates that the committee did not want to make the mistake of Governor Eberhart's commission, whose proposal for single-headed departments got such a cool reception. The committee had studied the Illinois and Ohio plans of single-headed departments and the Massachusetts and Pennsylvania multiple-headed departmental reorganizations, and apparently concluded that the former could be dangerous in the hands of a weak or corrupt governor. Governor Christianson was quoted as saying in one of his addresses: "We do not want a cabinet form of government, as in some states" (*Minneapolis Journal*, January 8, 1925). A well-known political news writer commented as follows: "One thing stands out in the Interim Committee report. The old conflict between a single department head and a board or commission is still on, but the three-man board has all the best of it" (*ibid.*, January 30, 1925).

[34] Of the three departments that the committee recommended placing under a single head, two, Agriculture and Highways, already were, and the third, Conserva-

ture was to be a new Department of Administration and Finance under the supervision of a three-man board that would serve at the pleasure of the governor. The committee recommended that all officials, departments, and agencies of the state be subject to the financial supervision of this department.

Under the plan this administrative commission would be composed of a comptroller, a commissioner of the budget, and a commissioner of purchases. The comptroller was to take over the postaudit duties of the public examiner and the responsibility for supervising state accounting, the budget commissioner was to have charge of budget preparation, and the purchasing commissioner was to operate a central purchasing system. The Printing Commission would be abolished and the new board would take over its duties. The committee recommended further that the board be directed to appoint a director of personnel who would administer a proposed civil service code, including a merit system for the selection of state employees.

The Commission of Administration and Finance was to be given complete authority to effect economies and efficiency through a quarterly allotment system, pre-audit of expenditures, supervision and control of all obligations incurred by state departments and agencies, and general powers of survey and investigation. The whole plan was designed to centralize related staff and control functions in one department and to give the governor the power, through the Commission of Administration and Finance, to limit and control expenditures in the interest of economy.[35]

Four of the five committee members signed the report. The fifth, Henry Spindler, the Farmer-Labor member, submitted a separate report in which he expressed general agreement with the aims and purposes of the majority.[36] He suggested that the greatest benefit in the proposed changes would come from an effective

tion, would consolidate several old departments, of which two, Drainage and Waters, and Game and Fish, were then each under a single commissioner.

[35] The evidence is unmistakable that the proposal for a fiscal control agency directly responsible to the governor was considered to be the heart of the reorganization plan. As one contemporary writer put it: "This department [Administration and Finance] is the crux of the whole interim plan. All the rest might go by the board, but if only this one department were created and given the powers outlined in the code, the state would be embarkd upon a wholly new system of administration" (*ibid.*, January 28, 1925). The governor as "general manager" and the plan as a "real revolution in state management" characterized the news comments of the day.

[36] Printed with the majority report in the same booklet.

budget system and unified purchasing and that the reshuffling of departments and divisions would not alone result in much economy. The minority report differed with the majority on the details of the reorganization, leaning even more to the board type of department and suggesting different allocations of some activities. He agreed in general with the plan for a Commission of Administration and Finance but suggested that the elective state auditor be a member of the board instead of creating the position of comptroller and that the postaudit be continued under an independent public examiner.

The Legislative Battle on the Reorganization Bill

A bill incorporating the recommendations of the majority of the Interim Committee was introduced concurrently in the House and Senate by the chairmen of the Civil Administration committees.[37] In the Senate several dozen amendments were proposed and accepted in committee. These changes reestablished a few departments and shifted their duties, adjusted some possible administrative conflicts, and weakened the civil service merit system provisions of the original bill. In the main these amendments were classed as friendly, they were not unacceptable to the backers of the bill, and they in no way weakened the main powers of the Commission of Administration and Finance. When the rewritten bill, incorporating the committee amendments, came up in the Senate on a special order on the afternoon of March 24, it appeared that it would almost certainly encounter strong and determined opposition.[38]

Reasons frequently cited for the strong Senate opposition to the reorganization bill were these: (1) The proposal came from a House committee rather than from a committee on which the Senate was represented; (2) the Senate had held over since the 1923 session and hence its members were not as close to the public desire for economy and reorganization as were the House members and the governor, both of whom had faced campaigns for votes in 1924;[39] (3) the upper chamber of the legislature was always

---

[37] H.F. 527 and S.F. 413.

[38] S.F. 674. The progress of the bill may be traced in the legislative journals.

[39] In Minnesota the entire House of Representatives is elected every two years, whereas the entire membership of the Senate is elected at four-year intervals, in the even years between presidential elections.

more conservative and less open to making changes than the lower house;[40] (4) Rockne, as chairman of the Senate Finance Committee, and Christianson, as chairman of the corresponding House committee, had fought on opposite sides of various legislative bills and proposals during preceding sessions of the legislature; (5) some members of the Senate Finance Committee resented the suggestion that economy in state government could not be achieved by their body without the aid of an administrative agency; (6) there was a desire to protect and preserve the complete independence of certain officials and departments, the executives or employees of which were close to certain senators; (7) the Farmer-Labor minority was naturally obliged to oppose the governor's major legislative proposal in order to be prepared for the 1926 campaign; and (8) a gubernatorial economy veto of a bill increasing certain local salaries threw four of the five senators from St. Louis County into the opposition.[41]

Eleven hostile amendments were proposed in the Senate and eight were adopted, most of them aimed at the Commission of Administration and Finance. The three most important changes proposed were these: one by A. J. Rockne enabling the Board of Control to retain all its powers, exempt from any supervision of the Commission of Administration and Finance; one by A. O. Devold wiping out the commission entirely and providing instead for a budget officer under an Executive Council of elective officials; and one by T. E. Sorenson exempting elective officials and their departments from all control of the commission. Both the Rockne and Devold amendments were once approved by the Senate, but supporters of the original bill managed to get new special orders twice to avoid final passage of the bill in such a mutilated condition.[42]

Debate on the bill was among the most intense the legislature had ever experienced; on several roll calls there were majorities

---

[40] This fact was already shown by the Senate's failure to concur in House proposals for interim committees on reorganization in 1911, 1913, 1921, and 1923, and by its failure to pass House bills for strengthening the budget system in 1919, 1921, and 1923. See above, pages 3, 7, and 8.

[41] *Minneapolis Journal*, March 22, 1925, and *Minneapolis Tribune*, April 1, 1925. In his inaugural message the governor had clearly indicated his opposition to local salary increases by the state legislature. See editorial questioning this policy in the *Minneapolis Journal*, March 23, 1925.

[42] The bill was debated on special orders in the Senate on March 24, March 31, and April 2.

of five, four, and even one.[43] A senator who had already left to accept an appointment to fill a vacancy in Congress returned to cast his vote on the measure; [44] another got up from a sickbed to vote; [45] and the governor took the unusual course of appealing through a radio speech to the electorate for support of the reorganization project.[46] Senator Rockne, veteran member of the upper house, fought one of his greatest battles, standing forth as "the spokesman for the 12,000 wards of Minnesota, those poor unfortunates whose voice can never be heard here." [47]

The two groups of Senate forces compromised and on April 2 passed an amended bill. As passed, the bill left the Board of Control independent in matters of purchasing and personnel for the state institutions, retained the plan for a Commission of Administration and Finance, but placed the commission "under supervision and jurisdiction" of an Executive Council of five elective officials.[48]

Meanwhile the House had revised its original bill in committee and introduced a new bill,[49] in substantially the same form as the original with respect to the proposed Commission of Administration and Finance, except that the civil service provisions, which had provoked an attack in committee, were omitted.[50] When the Senate bill reached the House, the contents of the House committee bill were substituted for the Senate provisions. Amendments simi-

[43] A Sullivan compromise amendment on purchasing lost 30–35; the second Rockne amendment on the Board of Control won 33–32; the Devold amendment lost 32–33, won 35–31 on a change of votes, was reconsidered by a vote of 34–33, and then won again by 34–33.

[44] Senator Allen J. Furlow of Rochester had been appointed Congressman from the first district and had already been excused for the balance of the legislative session. Since Congress was not in session, however, he had not been sworn in. His reappearance in the legislature caused heated remarks by the bill's opposition, and reportedly led some senators to join the opposition on the Devold amendment.

[45] Senator Sherman W. Child of Minneapolis. See the *Minneapolis Journal,* April 2, 1925.

[46] March 28. It was an unusual procedure in 1925.

[47] *Minneapolis Journal,* April 2, 1925. Rockne voiced the conviction that "if someone goes out to make a record for the state under this new plan, the wards of the state, who could not speak for themselves, might suffer" (*ibid.,* April 12, 1925). In other speeches, however, Rockne seemed to share the views of various other senators that the bill gave the governor too much power over the departments as well as the institutions.

[48] S.F. 674, Art. II, Sec. 4, as passed by the Senate on April 2, 1925, and unofficially printed for the House.

[49] H.F. 1337, introduced March 27, 1925.

[50] Action in the lower house was delayed by the serious illness of Representative W. I. Norton of Minneapolis, secretary of the Interim Committee and largely responsible for the drafting of the original bill. Norton, who was expected to lead the fight for the bill in the House, was not able to attend the sessions until April 7, 1925.

lar to the ones that the Senate had approved were easily defeated, and with only two minor changes in wording, the bill as revamped by the House committee was passed April 8 by the overwhelming vote of 110 to 16. This bill provided that the Department of Administration and Finance be strictly an agent of the governor, and it placed all state departments and institutions under its management in matters of finance and purchasing.

The Conference Committee Compromise

The Senate refused to concur in the changes that the House had made in the bill, and so it went to a Conference Committee composed of five members of each house. Choice of the Conference Committee lay with Lieutenant Governor W. I. Nolan and with the speaker of the house, both supporters of the bill. Accordingly, nine of the ten committee members favored the House draft of the bill,[51] while Senator Rockne was the sole committee member opposed to that draft. But the supporters of the bill feared that Rockne had sufficient Senate support to reject the conference report and thereby kill the bill itself, if he were beaten in the Conference Committee.

The Conference Committee, therefore, compromised with Rockne on his Board of Control proposal and agreed that the bill should exempt the personnel of the institutions from the supervision of the Commission of Administration and Finance and that the Board of Control should be permitted to purchase its own supplies for the maintenance and repair of the institutions, but under the general supervision of the commission. The Devold move to place the new commission under the Executive Council was rejected, however, and in general, except for the concession regarding the Board of Control, the Conference Committee's provisions with respect to the Commission of Administration and Finance followed the lines of the House bill.

The House promptly accepted the conference report on April 17 by a vote of 116 to 9; the nine negative votes came from eight Farmer-Laborites and one conservative. In the Senate the battle was not yet won, and only the alertness of the presiding officer, Lieutenant Governor Nolan, saved the bill. When the message from

[51] Senator C. H. MacKenzie and Representative O. K. Dahle, chairmen of the two Civil Administration committees, were chairmen of Senate and House conferees, respectively. These two men led the floor fight in favor of the administration bill.

the House stating that it had passed the bill as amended in conference reached the Senate, acrimonious debate occurred. Attempts were made to defeat the bill with motions to reject and to lay it on the table (only four working days remained in the session), but Nolan held them out of order in accordance with Senate rules that gave Conference Committee reports a privileged status. The opposition then moved to adjourn and won, 33 to 28. But Nolan ruled that the report would still be the first order of business the next day. When the battle was renewed, the struggle was less vigorous; the conference report was adopted, 37 to 29, and the bill was then repassed April 18 by a vote of 47 to 19. On final passage the opposition included Farmer-Labor members, some St. Louis County senators (still disgruntled over the governor's veto of the local salary increase), and some conservative opponents of the plan.[52]

But the 1925 legislature was not yet through hearing about the reorganization. On the last night of the session a serious deadlock occurred between the House and Senate on the big state department appropriation bill. Although the tie-up was due to a Senate rider increasing the salaries of the state auditor and state treasurer in defiance of the governor's economy plan, the governor and his program were the target of several verbal attacks on various subjects during the night. At one time a motion was offered to strike out from the bill the appropriation for the new Department of Administration and Finance, but it was ruled out of order. At last agreement was reached, the appropriations were passed, and the legislature adjourned. The governor wisely signed the reorganization bill only after all other bills had been signed, or vetoed, so that there would be no possibility it would be modified by a chance provision in some other bill that might become law after the reorganization act.

Over some of the most bitter opposition that any legislative

[52] Party lines on the reorganization bill in the Senate were badly broken. Farmer-Labor members, at first expressing some favor for the governor's proposals, later voiced dissatisfaction with the Interim Committee's report as concentrating too much power in the governor and promising little in the way of economy. Apparently their strategy was to seek the passage of damaging amendments that would kill the plan without assuming responsibility for its ultimate defeat. The *Minnesota Union Advocate* denounced the plan as a "monumental farce" that "neither simplifies the government nor gives assurance of economy," and that "puts the machinery of government pretty well in the hands of the chief executive, and makes him to a large extent the dispenser of vast political patronage" (quoted by C. B. Cheney in the *Minneapolis Journal*, February 11, 1925).

proposal had encountered in years, the Interim Committee plan for securing economy and efficiency in state government through a three-man Commission of Administration and Finance had become law. The original plan for the centralization of staff control functions had been weakened by certain exemptions for the Board of Control and the state institutions. The recommendations for the establishment of a merit system in the state civil service had been abandoned (without ever coming to a decisive vote on the floor) in favor of giving the new department only a few personnel powers. But the heart of the plan — giving the governor, through the commission, full control of the expenditures of all state departments and agencies by means of an allotment and pre-audit system — had been accepted by the legislature and written into law.

Chapter 2

POLITICAL AND LEGAL HISTORY
OF THE DEPARTMENT

DURING the entire fourteen years that the Commission of Administration and Finance was in existence it was a subject of political,
legislative, and judicial interest and action. The most prominent
characteristics of its history in this respect were these: (1) The
commission frequently clashed with other state executives and
administrators, especially the elective officials; (2) the commission
was often used by the opposition as a target for criticism directed
against the governor and the party in power; (3) there was continuous opposition to the commission in some legislative circles,
particularly in the Senate; and (4) the commission operated under
the handicap that its authority was dwindling continually.

The First Year

The choice of the right men to comprise the first Commission
of Administration and Finance was important; it took Governor
Christianson a month and a half after passage of the reorganization
act to decide upon his appointments and secure the consent of the
men whom he selected.[1] On June 16, 1925, the membership of
the new "super-board" or "Big Three," as the newspapers had
already dubbed it, was announced. Henry Rines had agreed to
resign from his position as state treasurer, which he had occupied
for eight and a half years, to become comptroller and chairman
of the new commission. A. J. Peterson of Dawson, generally regarded as the governor's personal appointee, was to be budget
commissioner. H. W. Austin, city purchasing agent of St. Paul,
was the choice for purchasing commissioner.

The new commission faced many problems in getting started.
Only two weeks remained until the beginning of the fiscal year,
when the reorganization act was supposed to be in operation; the
commission had to begin its work in makeshift offices in the already

[1] Newspaper reports intimated that the governor was experiencing some difficulty
in finding the type of businessman desired for the budget and purchasing jobs who
would consent to serve at the salary ($5,000) fixed in the statute (*St. Paul Dispatch*,
April 27, May 26, 1925).

crowded capitol; it had no organization, no trained employees, no equipment, no blank forms ready for use. It was faced with the double handicap that the public, led by the newspapers, was expecting early announcements of major economies and important moves in the direction of efficiency, while the various state departments, officials, and agencies were apprehensive and perhaps a little belligerent in yielding to the new department even a small part of the independence they had previously enjoyed.[2]

Members of the commission tackled their job promptly. An executive secretary was selected at once and a skeleton organization created. By the twentieth of June a request had been made of all departments for quarterly allotment estimates for the period beginning July 1 and for specific information as to the unpaid obligations of each department. A few days later the commission announced it would shortly undertake a general survey of all state departments to determine where economies might be instituted. During July the commission members made a brief trip east, where they examined the operation of central financial departments in several other states, and later in the year the executive secretary was sent to spend six weeks studying the work of the Massachusetts Commission on Administration and Finance.

It was almost inevitable that long-established departments would resent the efforts of the new commission to exercise supervision in the direction of economy. In the very first month of its existence disputes with two departments brought considerable newspaper publicity and set the pace for other departments to exhibit an uncooperative spirit. The first of these disputes was with the elective state auditor, Ray Chase, who had been made a member of the new Conservation Commission by the 1925 legislature. The Conservation Commission had decided to create the position of state park superintendent at a salary of $3,600 a year. In the quarterly allotment budget the Big Three disallowed the item. Charges and threats of defiance were hurled back and forth.[3]

[2] The high expectations held out to the people by the advocates of the reorganization act are revealed in the following editorial: "It is hoped the fact [beginning of the new system] will be a landmark of governmental progress to which the people of the state may look back with pride and satisfaction. . . . It is such a responsibility as no other governor of Minnesota ever had. The manner of its discharge by him and those under him will go far to determine the standards of future administrations" (*Minneapolis Tribune*, July 1, 1925).

[3] One newspaper called it "open warfare" and said one of Chase's letters was "filled with dynamite" (*St. Paul Daily News*, July 21, 1925). Another newspaper said that

The deputy state auditor helped the controversy along by announcing that because of the Big Three two thousand state employees had no prospect of getting salary checks for days to come and that tardiness in the handling of expenses had cost the state several thousand dollars worth of cash discounts in the first two weeks of July.[4] Chase added fuel to the fire by criticizing the commission for its trip east and by questioning their action with respect to the budgets of other departments.[5]

A second major controversy arose with the Minnesota Railroad and Warehouse Commission. That commission, an elective body, not only claimed that the grain inspection fund, arising out of their major activity, was not subject to the quarterly allotment or to other supervision of the Big Three but also protested the action of the Big Three in disallowing a few salary increases for employees paid from other funds of the department. The Commission of Administration and Finance had taken the general position that, in the interests of economy, salary increases should not be made immediately but should wait until the commission had an opportunity for further study of the pay-roll situation. The controversy was carried to the Supreme Court for a final decision. The court ruled[6] that the Railroad and Warehouse Commission was in all respects subject to the supervision of the Commission of Administration and Finance, but it also held that the salary-fixing power given to the Big Three by the reorganization act was to be exercised in conjunction with the adoption of a classification and compensation plan. Since the commission had not as yet had the time to make a survey, prepare a classification plan, and adopt salary schedules, its action in attempting to disallow a certain salary increase was held improper.

Chase's caustic letter to the Big Three was "the most sensational letter sent in many years by an elective state official to any agency of the Minnesota government" (*St. Paul Dispatch*, July 21, 1925).

[4] *Minneapolis Journal*, July 19, 1925.

[5] With respect to the trip east, Chase is quoted in the newspapers as saying, "This department has been in office 18 days. It has now started for Boston. It might better have remained in St. Paul attending to matters that are of Minnesota importance. Our state government is far superior to that of Massachusetts and it is needless to make these junkets at the expense of the state. The accounting systems there are out of date. There are many other states where more efficient accounting systems are in effect and Minnesota is one of them" (*St. Paul Dispatch*, July 20, 1925). The *St. Paul Daily News* tried to minimize the importance of the argument in an editorial (July 22, 1925) in which it asserted that it was a scheme of "old-timers" to discredit the governor, and it suggested that Chase had gubernatorial ambitions himself.

[6] State ex rel. Yapp *et al.* v. Ray P. Chase *et al.*, 165 Minn. 268 (1925).

21

179549

The governor took no direct part in these early controversies. He made a public statement, pointing out that some frictions would naturally develop in putting the reorganization act into operation and suggesting that such disputes should not be regarded seriously. By the end of the first year the Big Three had completed its organization and set the precedents for its future operations. The quarterly allotment system was in operation, budgetary accounting records were being kept, major contracts were coming to the department for approval, a personnel survey had been instituted, the purchasing division was buying supplies, material, and equipment when requested by departments, and the printing and public examining divisions were carrying on in substantially the same manner as before 1925. The commission itself was free to devote a good share of its time to problems of economy and efficiency.

The 1926 Campaign and the 1927 Legislature

The gubernatorial campaign in 1926 was certain to be the popular testing ground of the Big Three. Two years earlier Christianson had been elected governor on a platform of reorganization and economy. The legislature had enacted into law a reorganization bill that provided in the Commission of Administration and Finance an agency enabling the governor to secure economy. The 1926 campaign issue was ready-made.

George E. Leach, mayor of Minneapolis, conducted a vigorous but unsuccessful campaign against Christianson for the Republican nomination. Leach launched a strong attack on the Big Three, calling it a clumsy, extravagant super-board, destructive to a cooperative spirit among state officials, and recommending its abolition.[7] In the campaign leading up to the general election Magnus Johnson, Farmer-Labor candidate, attacked the Big Three on the ground that it had too much power and intimated that no appointive board should exercise powers superior to those of elective officials.[8]

[7] In contrast he suggested: "A Director of the Budget has satisfied the needs of the United States government. A 'Director of the Budget' can solve the economic problems of Minnesota. I favor the establishment of such an office" (opening address of George E. Leach, candidate for governor in 1926, printed in pamphlet form).

[8] Not all Farmer-Laborites opposed the governor on this issue, however. Hjalmar Petersen, an active leader in that party, writing in the *Askov American* on May 6, 1926, commented: "Mr. Christianson stands well with the country folks and thinkers generally because he means what he says and there is something back of his economy program."

Governor Christianson put up a strong campaign on the claim that he had kept his promise of two years ago. By use of the veto power he had at last stopped the marked upward trend in appropriations. Through the steps thus far taken for reorganization of the administrative structure a more efficient state government had come into being, and through the actions of the new "budget board" vast savings had been achieved. Quoting a figure of $683,579 [9] as the savings effected by the new board the governor cited example after example of economies — not only through allotment reductions but in purchases of coal, gasoline, and license tags, in the telephone contract, and in printing. He pledged himself to continue to hold appropriations down and to effect further economies,[10] and he pointed to a vision of a "bondless and taxless state" in the future.[11] Christianson was reelected by a vote of 395,779 to 266,845 for Johnson.

The larger part of the governor's 1927 inaugural address was devoted to a discussion of the need for further economy in public expenditures. He again promised not to approve increased appropriations. Speaking of civil administration Christianson suggested that the task of reorganization was not yet complete, and recommended, among other changes, that the purchasing activities of the Board of Control be transferred to the Department of Administration and Finance.[12]

But the Big Three had yet to face its first legislative session. And the Senate, which had been so wary of creating the new department two years earlier, was not kindly disposed toward it. The commission's first budget document had been delayed and was not ready at the opening of the session; the Senate Finance Committee raised a cry that the Big Three was stalling. The Senate refused to let the Commission of Administration and Finance handle its print-

[9] A study of the method used in arriving at this figure shows it was hardly an accurate indication of savings due solely to the Big Three.

[10] "The budget system should save more money during the second year than during the first; more during the third year than during the second. Reducing expenditures does not involve any spectacular achievement; it does not make good first-page copy. It consists in finding the thousands of small items of extravagance and stopping them. It consists of making every dollar of tax money render one hundred cents of service" (keynote address opening the primary campaign, May 12, 1936).

[11] "A bondless and taxless state — taxless so far as direct levy for revenue fund purposes are concerned — is the objective in the attainment of which I invite the participation of the people in Minnesota" (keynote address in the general election campaign, September 28, 1936).

[12] Second Inaugural Message of Governor Theodore Christianson, January 5, 1927, p. 15.

ing, though the House had agreed to do so. The governor's suggestion that the Board of Control's purchasing activities be consolidated with those of the central purchasing division brought forth a barrage of Senate criticism that quickly squelched the plan. Disgruntled department heads were quick to carry their tales of criticism to legislators, who heard them readily. And when the biennial budget was given to the legislature, several weeks late, the Senate Finance Committee chose to ignore it as far as possible. Although the House was much more sympathetic than the Senate, it joined with the senators in voting increased appropriations for the Board of Control and for educational purposes, which the governor found it necessary to veto in order to save his budget plan.

Embezzlement of money by the deputy state treasurer and a system of forging state warrants by an employee in the state auditor's office and an employee in the treasurer's office had recently been brought to light, and the legislature decided that there should be a thorough audit of the auditor's and treasurer's offices. Since the public examining division was under direction of the comptroller, who had been state treasurer while part of the shortages had occurred,[13] it was decided to authorize an independent audit under direction of the attorney general, and an appropriation of $25,000 was made to finance it. A firm of certified public accountants performed the audit but reported that the state's accounting records in the auditor's office were in such a deplorable state that it was impossible even to determine certain elementary facts, such as the amount of warrants outstanding. A complete revision of accounting practices was urgently recommended.[14] No action resulted.

The Big Three weathered the legislative storm without losing any of its powers, but rough waters were still ahead. Difficulties with departments and criticisms of the "super-board" continued. The auditor discarded some new machine accounting records that the comptroller had installed in his office a year earlier; the Game and Fish Department questioned the commission's authority over fishing contracts; and the Livestock Sanitary Board instituted a suit in district court over the Big Three's action in abolishing one of the positions in the board's employ.[15] On June 30, 1927, the com-

---

[13] No hint of blame was attached to Mr. Rines, however.

[14] Report of the examination by Hines and Bachmann, Certified Public Accountants (477 typed pages), January 16, 1928.

[15] Apparently the action of the commission resulted from a controversy over the appointment of a quarantine officer. The suit was dismissed when the executive secre-

mission promulgated its new classification of state employees and maximum salary schedules to accompany it; employees throughout the state service who found in this move a restriction upon future salary increases were quick to criticize the new rules of the Big Three.

Throughout the legislative session and in the midst of disputes with departments Governor Christianson gave the commission his full backing, but the commission, not the governor, was usually the target of criticism.

The University Lawsuit

Controversy was also brewing between the university and the Commission of Administration and Finance over the extent of the Big Three's control. The Big Three had actually undertaken only a minimum of financial supervision over actions of the university regents.[16] The allotment system and the approval of contracts were the only major controls exercised. Under the allotment system the Big Three required a breakdown of estimated expenditures from the maintenance appropriation into only a few major items—usually salaries, supplies and expense, capital outlay, and miscellaneous. It was the practice of the first Commission of Administration and Finance to approve allotments for customary and usual activities as a matter of course, but proposed increased expenditures or proposed expenditures for new activities were closely scrutinized.

Twice the Big Three refused to approve proposals of the university for new projects. Once the university wanted to embark upon a program of providing group insurance for its staff members, involving an initial outlay of $45,000. The commission disallowed the item for this purpose in the quarterly allotment request, holding that since the legislature had at various times refused to establish retirement funds for other state employees the commission should not and could not properly consent to the creation of a system of group insurance at the university, the cost of which would probably be reflected in increased appropriation needs in the future. The other disagreement came over the plan of the university regents to

tary of the Livestock Sanitary Board, Dr. C. E. Cotton, was permitted to retain the man he had appointed as quarantine officer (*St. Paul Dispatch*, September 28, 1927).

[16] The university did not question the budget-making as distinguished from the budget-enforcing powers of the Big Three. In the matter of purchasing, the university was permitted to do its own buying, but cooperation was effected in the procurement of large bulk purchases, such as coal and light bulbs. This cooperation continued after the university was exempted by judicial decision from Big Three control.

pledge the credit of the university to build dormitories. The Big Three declined to give its approval on the ground that the legislature at its 1925 session had refused to authorize the dormitory plan and hence an administrative body would be presumptuous to sanction it.[17] The university decided to make the group insurance controversy a case to test the authority of the commission to veto expenditures authorized by the board of regents.[18]

Marshaling its best talent, including the dean of its law school, the university presented a well-prepared case, arguing that the reorganization act was unconstitutional, at least so far as it attempted to restrict the regents in their powers of exclusive management of the university. It was pointed out that the state constitution, adopted in 1857, had created the university as a constitutional corporation and had perpetuated unto the university all the rights previously granted by territorial laws. This prevented the legislature from interfering with the university management by placing any other body in a supervisory position over university finances, it was claimed. It was also argued that the reorganization act was unconstitutional because in effect it extended the veto power of the governor over appropriations, was a delegation of legislative powers, had a faulty title, and was otherwise defective.

The attorney general's office defended the Commission of Administration and Finance and the reorganization act. Against the argument of the university's special, constitutionally granted privileges it was pointed out that for more than sixty-five years the legislature had passed numerous acts pertaining to the organization and management of the university and that the university had consented to and abided by such laws. In further defense of the constitutionality of the reorganization act, the attorney general said that in effect the act created no new powers over expenditures but only transferred part of the power to curtail expenditures from one executive or administrative official to another; department heads were not bound by law to expend every cent of appropriations, he argued, and the legislature had a right to transfer from one official to others the authority to restrict spending.

[17] Christianson set forth the Big Three's views on these two matters in his 1929 inaugural address, pp. 13–14.

[18] Governor Christianson later pointed out in his *Minnesota: A History of the State and Its People* ([5 vols., Chicago, 1935], 2: 476–77), that had he desired to control university policy he could have done so through his power to appoint the regents (he had appointed nine of the ten members of the board).

The Supreme Court handed down its decision on July 27, 1928.[19] It held that the reorganization act intended to subject all agencies of the state government to financial control of the governor through the Commission of Administration and Finance, and that the court would not interfere with such a decision of legislative policy except as it might contravene constitutional limitations. But the constitution had made the university independent of all other executive authority, the court said, and therefore, to the extent that the reorganization act attempted to subject the control of the university finances to the supervision of the Big Three, it was unconstitutional. The decision turned entirely upon the university's special status as a constitutional corporation [20] and in no way restricted or limited the Big Three's powers of supervision and control over other departments and agencies of the state.

The Last Three Years under Christianson

The Big Three won an unqualified victory in two other Supreme Court decisions in 1928; both were suits over highway contracts. The highway commissioner attempted to award a contract to one bidder; the Big Three refused to approve the award and determined that another bidder was lower. The controversy began over a misplaced decimal point, but it resolved itself into a question of whether or not final authority to approve or disapprove highway contracts rested with the Big Three. The highway commissioner claimed exclusive power to award the contracts, but the court ruled that the reorganization act prevailed and that the Big Three's supervision and control extended to all highway contracts.[21]

[19] State ex rel. University of Minnesota et al. v. Ray P. Chase, 175 Minn. 259 (1928). Technically the Commission of Administration and Finance was not a party to the suit. The action was a petition for mandamus to require Chase, the state auditor, to approve a voucher and issue a warrant for fifty dollars in payment of an item of expense incurred in connection with installing the group insurance plan, which Chase refused to do, since the voucher did not have the approval of the Big Three.

[20] The lower court had not only ruled that the university was free from the financial control and supervision of the Big Three but inferred that the reorganization act was invalid also in so far as it conflicted with the powers of other constitutional officers and agencies, such as the state auditor (St. Paul Dispatch, February 8, 1928). The decision had far-reaching effects upon the university itself: It threw the university back upon its territorial charter, made necessary the legislative election of the board of regents, and changed the relation of the president to the board. Cf. Fanning et al. v. University of Minnesota et al., 183 Minn. 222 (1931), and State ex rel. Peterson v. Quinlivan, 198 Minn. 65 (1936).

[21] State ex rel. J. J. Mergens et al. v. Charles M. Babcock et al., 175 Minn. 583 (1928); State ex rel. Charles Weaver v. Charles M. Babcock, 175 Minn. 590 (1928). The lower court had ruled against the Big Three (St. Paul Dispatch, April 13, 1928).

COMMISSION OF ADMINISTRATION AND FINANCE

The governor campaigned for reelection again in 1928 on a four-point platform: continuation of the economy program, standing by the budget system and strengthening it, planning for a better conservation program, and promoting the cause of agriculture.[22] He pledged himself to continue along the lines of economy and he put up a vigorous defense of the Big Three and the allotment system. Farmer-Laborites, whose vote in the general election was their lowest in a decade, said "Christianson's economy administration is a myth." [23] Andrew Nelson, Democratic candidate for governor, made "repeal of the so-called Reorganization Act" number one on his list of "much needed reform measures." [24] Christianson was returned an easy victor with 549,857 votes, as compared to 227,193 for his nearest opponent.

The necessity for discussing numerous items of proposed legislation in the 1929 inaugural did not deter the governor from again calling the attention of the legislature to budget problems. He announced that an increase in the population of state institutions made necessary some increases in appropriations. But the budget as a whole, though not as low as the preceding one, was conservative in its recommendations.

Controversy arose over the recommended educational appropriations. The commission had made a special study of the university budget, including a salary comparison covering a period of years and an investigation of the diversion of part of the maintenance appropriation to enlarge the plant. On the basis of their study, only a small increase in the university appropriation was recommended. University officials, faced with a growing institution, called a strong lobby of alumni, students, students' relatives, and educators into action to get a much larger increase.[25] Inconsistencies and misrepresentations were charged by both sides.

The House committee, after a study of the accounts, set their appropriation figure for the university even below that of the executive budget; the Senate committee sided with the university, and the Senate got the best of the compromise. At the same time the Senate gave strong support to an increase in the appropriations for

[22] From Governor Theodore Christianson's address at Hutchinson, Minnesota, October 2, 1928, formally opening his campaign for reelection.
[23] From a circular issued on behalf of the Farmer-Labor candidates, 1928.
[24] Folder entitled "Andrew Nelson's Pledges to the People of the State," 1928.
[25] Harold E. Stassen, later the governor in whose administration the Big Three was abolished, was one of the student leaders in the fight for larger university appropriations in 1929.

state aid to public schools. When the educational appropriation bill reached the governor, he adhered to the budget and his earlier economy pledges by using his veto power to strike out the increased appropriations for the university and the public schools; the rest of the bill was approved and became law. This strengthened the economy bloc and created uncertainty in the legislature as to the correct procedure to follow in attempting to override an item veto on a bill that had already become law. These factors, together with the rapid approach of the time for adjournment, influenced the legislators to compromise and pass a new bill acceptable to the governor, appropriating for these two educational items only $50,000 more than the Big Three had recommended.

The 1929 legislature passed an act providing for the erection of a state office building near the capitol. Since the Commission of Administration and Finance had been in charge of all state building construction after 1925, it would normally have been placed in control of this new project, and the Public Buildings Committee of the House so recommended. But it was suggested in the Senate that a State Office Building Commission be created for the purpose. The governor, anxious to placate some of the political leaders, agreed to the Senate proposal and the bill was so passed. When time came for appointment of the building commission, the governor designated the members of the Big Three to three of the seven positions.

The 1930 campaign was one of the hottest in Minnesota's history. Governor Christianson and Senator Thomas D. Schall drew the attention and votes of members of all parties in the race for the Republican nomination for United States Senator. Schall did not hesitate to use his congressional franking privilege, covering the state with startling attacks on all aspects of Christianson's administrations, including the Big Three.[26] The governor was defeated and in the fall Schall was reelected.

For the first time in a number of years state budget matters were not a primary issue in the gubernatorial contest, which lay between Ray P. Chase, Republican, state auditor, and Floyd B. Olson, Farmer-Labor, Hennepin County attorney. Both candidates promised economy in state administration, but the campaign cen-

[26] With relation to economy and reorganization Schall claimed that there were 40,000 state employees (at least 30,000 more than official figures revealed) and that "there has been economy wherever widows and orphans and the insane are concerned." Christianson answered that there had been an increase in welfare and institution appropriations during his administration.

tered around other issues brought on by the depression, such as the collapse in securities, problems of law enforcement, and a growing sense of the need for new policies of land use. On the subject of the Big Three, Chase in his keynote address recommended "minor amendments" to the reorganization act in order to eliminate irritation and define more clearly the limits of authority.[27] Olson, whose political astuteness made him realize that the people did not have a strong interest in such a subject at the time, said nothing. The final count of votes revealed that the state had elected its first Farmer-Labor governor, but that the Republicans had elected other state officials and that the conservative element would control both houses of the 1931 legislature.

The First Olson Commission

During the first year in office Governor Olson gradually replaced the members of the Commission of Administration and Finance with new appointees who he thought would be more sympathetic with the aims and purposes of his administration. Upon the expiration of Rines's term as comptroller on February 1, 1931, E. J. Pearlove was appointed to that post. On March 15 Mrs. Jean Wittich became budget commissioner and on October 1 Carl R. Erickson became purchasing commissioner.[28] The new commission, bringing fresh viewpoints to its work, found some hitherto undiscovered leaks in the expenditure of state moneys and stopped them, seized some opportunities for effecting economies in departmental operations, and devoted considerable attention to an expanded program of building construction to which the governor was committed, both in order to meet neglected needs of the state institutions and to provide public works as a method of combating the growing depression.[29]

[27] Chase was in a dilemma; as state auditor he had clashed with the Big Three probably more often than any other state official, but as the leader of the Republican ticket, he was committed to support the major achievements of the outgoing Republican governor. Olson's failure to carry on the traditional Farmer-Labor attack against the Christianson economy and reorganization program was probably influenced by the fact that Mrs. Jean Wittich was chairman of the "all-party" committee in charge of his campaign. Mrs. Wittich had given the reorganization act a large measure of active support, both before and after its passage, as a leader in the Minnesota League of Women Voters.

[28] Rines had sought the Republican nomination for state auditor in 1930 on an economy platform but was defeated. Austin, purchasing commissioner, resigned after denying the charge that he had failed to cooperate with the new administration (*St. Paul Dispatch*, April 28, 1930, September 9, 10, 1931).

[29] In September 1932 the administration was able to boast that, in addition to a large highway program made possible by a heavy bond issue, the state had let con-

Budget matters received considerable attention during the biennium of 1931–33. Efforts to economize, including a "payless vacation" plan in 1932, brought the Big Three a good deal of attention. This was followed by the presentation of the biennial budget to the 1933 legislature. It was much different from the previous budgets. Mimeographed in order to save money, brightened by pictures, graphs, and quotations on politics and government, Mrs. Wittich's budget attempted to tackle and solve the heavy financial problems facing the state. For the first time a Minnesota budget included all the funds in the state treasury and attempted to point out methods of financing the recommended appropriations. The budget proved to be interesting to the state legislators and the public, but some of the recommendations, especially those pertaining to a proposed shift in the use of certain revenues, were too novel to receive serious consideration.

During the first years of the Olson administration the commission encountered various difficulties with the elective officials. The new state auditor, Stafford King, and Comptroller Pearlove clashed over the respective powers of the two offices on matters of auditing claims and accounting. The state treasurer, Julius Schmahl, was irked by the methods that the Big Three used in checking and auditing his records, and a little later he retaliated by creating a stir over an expense account of one of the commission's members.[30] The secretary of state was not particularly pleased with the comptroller's suggestion, made to the 1933 legislature, that the principal portion of the secretary of state's office, the motor vehicle division, be transferred to the Department of Highways.[31] The attorney general not only took the side of the state auditor in his dispute with the Big Three but intervened in taxpayers' lawsuits against the Commission of Administration and Finance and the commissioner of highways.

A group of six highway lawsuits went to the Supreme Court for decision. In taking bids for certain construction work the Highway Department had limited the bidding to certain firms, and grossly excessive bids resulted. The department let the contracts, however, with the nominal approval of the Big Three. Taxpayers' suits were instituted, charging collusion and fraud and asking the court to de-

tracts for buildings and improvements amounting to $4,516,973.79 in 1931 and the first eight months of 1932, as compared to only $2,115,439.27 in the calendar years 1929 and 1930.

[30] St. Paul Dispatch, September 11, 1931, August 31, 1932.

[31] Ibid., February 8, 1933.

clare the contracts void. The attorney general, representing the state, appeared as an intervenor on the side of the taxpayers. Although the blame originally was attached primarily to the contractors and the Highway Department, the Commission of Administration and Finance was a subject of criticism when it agreed by stipulation with the attorney general and the contractors that the work already begun under the contracts should be continued and that 80 per cent of the contract price be paid when it was completed, the remaining 20 per cent to be held in abeyance until settlement of the case in the courts. The Supreme Court held that the contracts were void and that there was no authority to stipulate the performance of a void contract.[32]

The Commission of Administration and Finance also became a target of the Democratic candidate for governor in the 1932 campaign. He charged that the cost of state government had increased more than twenty-five million dollars a year since the 1925 reorganization act had been passed, and asked for the abolition of the Big Three.[33] The race lay between the Republican and Farmer-Labor candidates, however, and Governor Olson was reelected by a substantial majority. Governor Olson came to the defense of the Big Three early in 1933, when Representative Hitchcock, conservative House leader, introduced a bill to abolish the commission.[34]

Internal difficulties beset the Commission of Administration and Finance during this entire period. A comptroller's audit of some purchasing transactions resulted in the discharge of Commissioner Austin's assistant. Friction developed in the comptroller's office, the chief public examiner was demoted, and the comptroller took over the duties of the position himself. The state printer who had been appointed by the new Big Three after Governor Olson assumed office took issue with the commission on certain matters pertaining to the conduct of his office and he was discharged. On top of these

[32] John J. Regan *et al.* v. Charles M. Babcock *et al.*, 188 Minn. 192 (1933).

[33] *St. Paul Dispatch*, June 15, 1932. Disbursements had increased by the amount claimed, but the additional expenditures were mainly due to increased state aids to local units of government and to new state activities authorized by legislative enactment.

[34] In a newspaper interview Governor Olson was quoted as asking the following questions: "In eliminating the Big Three is Mr. Hitchcock opposed to the centralized purchasing department which has saved thousands of dollars for the taxpayers? Is he in favor of eliminating the state budget? Does he believe there should be no state comptroller to supervise and investigate expenditures by local subdivisions of government?" (*St. Paul Dispatch*, January 12, 1933.)

difficulties a difference of opinion developed within the commission itself. Several two-to-one votes on important matters were followed by the refusal of the other two commissioners to approve the budget prepared by Mrs. Wittich in January 1933.[35] This was the climax to the friction within the commission, and shortly afterwards Mrs. Wittich announced she would resign at the conclusion of the legislative session.[36] On May 15 Governor Olson appointed I. C. Strout, director of the Farmer-Labor Educational Bureau, to fill the position of budget commissioner and director of personnel.

A New Trend in the Attorney General's Opinions

With the political changes that occurred in 1931 there came a halt to the attorney general's opinions favorable to the Big Three, and even after 1933 the consistently favorable interpretations of the law that had prevailed in earlier years were replaced with somewhat unfavorable ones.

From 1925 to 1931 the attorney general's office had consistently held that the commission's powers extended to all agencies of state government, then existing or thereafter created, except where the law expressly exempted a department or agency from its supervision in some respect. Opinions held that the Big Three's allotment control extended to the grain inspection fund of the Railroad and Warehouse Commission, even though some legislators thought it had been exempted when the 1925 act was passed; to the Metropolitan Drainage Commission, which was financed primarily by the two largest cities; and to the Upper Mississippi and St. Croix River Improvement Commission, created in 1927 and not specifically made subject to the 1925 act by statute.[37]

The attorney general also rendered opinions that the comptroller had the authority to prescribe the kind of records and accounts to be used in the auditor's and treasurer's offices; that a contract between the Board of Control and an engineer could be terminated by the Big Three despite contrary provisions in the contract; that even renewal options of contracts were subject to approval by the Commission of Administration and Finance; and that the classification and compensation fixing powers of the Big Three extended to em-

[35] "Minutes of the Commission," Book B, p. 718 (January 13, 1933).
[36] *St. Paul Dispatch*, March 11, 1933.
[37] Opinions of August 11, 1925, August 23, 1927, and January 24, 1928, respectively. J. E. Markham, an assistant attorney general during this period, had assisted members of the Interim Committee in drafting the reorganization act.

ployees whose positions had been established with a given compensation by statute before 1925.[38]

He further held that a 1927 law, apparently bestowing upon the game and fish commissioner the power to contract for removal and sale of rough fish from state waters, did not repeal or suspend in any way the operation of the 1925 reorganization act and that therefore such contracts were still to be made under the supervision and control of the Big Three.[39] In 1929, in an opinion involving an act of that year relating to the Board of Medical Examiners, the attorney general held that as a matter of statutory construction a new statute did not affect or suspend operations of an older one any further than the plain terms of the new statute required, and that therefore the reorganization act of 1925 should be construed as applicable to all departments, whether then existing or thereafter created.[40]

Up to 1931 the three Supreme Court decisions on the powers of the Big Three had all held that the purpose of the reorganization act was to give the Commission of Administration and Finance financial supervision and control over all agencies of the state, and that this intention was to be carried out, except as restricted by constitutional limitations in the case of the university.[41] In a fourth decision late in 1931 the court held the same thesis in even stronger language than before.[42]

Shortly after Stafford King (Republican) became state auditor and Pearlove (Farmer-Labor) was appointed comptroller in 1931, King asked the attorney general, Henry Benson (Republican), for an advisory opinion as to the respective powers and duties of the auditor and comptroller. In a lengthy reply Benson cast doubts upon the constitutionality of the reorganization act, in so far as it attempted to give to the comptroller greater powers than it gave to the elective auditor with respect to accounting or pre-auditing functions.

From 1933 through 1938, when Farmer-Laborites held the office of attorney general, a series of opinions exempted such agencies as

[38] Opinions of April 22, 1926, August 18, 1925, May 27, 1929, and December 23, 1925.
[39] Opinion of August 18, 1927.
[40] Opinion of November 27, 1929.
[41] State ex rel. Thomas Yapp et al. v. Ray P. Chase et al., 165 Minn. 268 (1925); State ex rel. University of Minnesota et al. v. Ray P. Chase, 175 Minn. 259 (1928); State ex rel. J. J. Mergens et al. v. Charles M. Babcock et al., 175 Minn. 583 (1928).
[42] State ex rel. William H. Kinler v. Henry Rines, 185 Minn. 49 (1931).

the important Rural Credit Department, the Board of Medical Examiners, and the Minneapolis–St. Paul Sanitary District, and the large expenditures of the State Relief Agency from supervision and control of the Commission of Administration and Finance.[43] In each case the exemption was based on the fact that the law creating or recreating the agency in question did not mention the 1925 reorganization act, and therefore, it was reasoned, the 1925 act did not apply. In 1936 a dispute arose between the attorney general and the Big Three when the attorney general refused to approve the form of a contract for installation and operation of a dial-telephone system in the capitol buildings.[44] The automatic system was subsequently installed in all offices except the attorney general's, but only after that officer had gone to court, secured a temporary injunction, and attempted to get a permanent injunction against execution of the contract.

When an investigation of the Bemidji Teachers' College building project occurred in 1938, the question of advertising for bids on state purchases was raised. The attorney general held that the language of the reorganization act that said the Commission of Administration and Finance " may make rules, regulations, and orders " for all state purchases, including provisions for advertisement for bids except when purchases were less than $500, made it mandatory to publish a newspaper advertisement for bids on purchases of $500 or more.[45] Since neither the Commission of Administration and Finance nor any other state agency had followed this practice in the past, the opinion was startling in its implication that many purchases made by the Big Three were illegal. In further opinions, however, the attorney general successively exempted from the advertising require-

[43] Opinions of May 24, October 24, 1933, April 15, July 2, November 10, 1936.
[44] The attorney general's approval as to form was required of all state contracts. He did not object to the form of this contract, however, but to its contents (letter of October 25, 1935). The 1933 legislature had appropriated $47,000 to the commission for purchase and installation of automatic telephone equipment; in several years of effort the commission found it impossible to purchase such potential equipment from manufacturers. Accordingly the appropriation was allowed to lapse, and the commission entered into a contract with the local telephone company in St. Paul to change the regular (rented) manual-telephone equipment in the capitol over to a dial basis. The Department of Public Property would continue to pay the central switchboard expense under the contract, and departments would continue to pay for the extensions, lines, and any other telephone equipment they used. The total cost under the new contract was less than under the manual system, though the cost for a few departments (including the attorney general) would be higher because of the particular equipment they desired.
[45] Opinion of July 23, 1938.

ment the purchases made by the State Relief Agency, the University of Minnesota, the State Board of Control, the Department of Highways, the Rural Credit Department, and the state treasurer's purchase of liquor stamps.[46]

Possible factors influencing the unfavorable opinions during the period 1933 through 1938, when the officials were members of the same political party, include friction between elective and appointive officials; differences arising from the comptroller's power to audit financial transactions to determine their legality, a function that bordered on the attorney general's power "to settle" legal questions for public officials; controversies between the state printer and the attorney general on the cost of printing the attorney general's reports; and clashes of personality between the persons concerned.

The 1935 Senate Inquiry

During the period 1933 to 1935 the commission functioned rather smoothly as far as internal organization was concerned. Each commissioner took care of the duties within his particular sphere of influence without interference from the others. Most active was the personnel division, which was engaged in formulating a new classification and compensation plan for state employees and which at the same time was coordinating and centralizing the handling of political patronage. On the matter of patronage Commissioner Strout, who was also serving as director of the Educational Bureau of the Farmer-Labor Association, wrote a letter to ninety newly appointed county and area foremen of the Highway Department that ostensibly imposed political obligations on these men in addition to their official duties.[47] A copy of the letter fell into other hands, a photograph of it was published in the newspapers, and a stir was created.

[46] Opinions of August 8, 1939 (State Relief Agency); August 11, 1938 (University of Minnesota); August 19, 1938 (Board of Control); August 31, 1938 (Department of Highways); September 13, 1938 (Rural Credits). The original opinion held that the law required the commission to make rules governing all state purchasing, but the later opinions modified it in effect to hold that the commission's rules were to apply only to the purchases by the commission itself.

[47] Excerpts from the letter read: "Quite recently you received the appointment as foreman for the State Department of Highways not only because of your ability to perform the services required but more particularly because of the fact that you were given the preferred endorsement of your County Farmer-Labor Association organization. . . . The State Committee of the Farmer-Labor Association on organization and education feels that when you accepted this appointment you also accepted the moral obligation to take the initiative in completing the organization work of the Farmer-Labor organization in your territory. . . ." The letter is reprinted in full on pages 38–39 of the majority report of the investigating committee, referred to below.

This, together with grumblings about the state relief adminis-tration and the conduct of the Highway Department, prompted the state Senate in 1935, which was in opposition to the governor, to appoint a committee of nine to investigate state departments. Dur-ing the legislative session the committee held a series of public hear-ings, at which an attorney selected by the committee examined witnesses of the committee's choosing. No cross-examination was permitted, however; witnesses were denied an opportunity to make statements or introduce evidence except in direct answer to ques-tions; and some persons who volunteered to give information were never called as witnesses. The eight majority members of the com-mittee submitted one report; [48] the lone minority committee member submitted another.[49]

The majority report charged not only that Strout was active in promoting political activity among state employees, but that he went over the heads of departments in placing applicants and dis-charging employees and that he was unfamiliar with his own budget document. They also charged Pearlove, the commission's chairman, with lack of detailed knowledge of actions taken by the commission and with being active in arranging for a "private dining room" in the capitol basement. Erickson was severely criticized for purchas-ing supplies at excessive prices, for buying inferior coal, and for soliciting business for certain railroad companies. The committee also cast a suspicion that irregularities existed in the manner of making purchases, and it pointed out that the failure of the Big Three to function as a deliberative commission was partly responsible for the conditions it found. It recommended that either the com-mission should constitute itself as a deliberative, working body, or it should be abolished and replaced with one responsible finance officer.[50]

[48] *Report of Investigating Committee of the Senate Created Under Resolution No. 2, For the Purpose of Investigating All Departments of the State Government of Minnesota: James A. Carley, Chairman, 1935.* Of the fifty-seven pages comprising the report sixteen are devoted to glaring irregularities in the state relief administra-tion, twenty-one to a number of serious charges against the Highway Department, sixteen to the Commission of Administration and Finance, less than a page to the Education Department, and three pages to "summary and recommended action."
[49] *Report of Investigating Committee of the Senate Created Under Resolution No. 2, For the Purpose of Investigating All Departments of the State Government of Minnesota: Individual Report of Senator Richard N. Gardner, 1935.*
[50] "Your committee was unable to find any indication of any coordinated action by the three Commissioners. . . . They seemed to act independently in their own respective departments" (*Report of Investigating Committee* [majority report], pp. 37–38).
"They [the Big Three] should constitute a deliberative and intelligent working

COMMISSION OF ADMINISTRATION AND FINANCE

The minority report charged that the "investigation was a fishing expedition," [51] motivated solely for political purposes. It agreed that Strout's letter to the highway foremen could be a subject of just criticism, but it upheld the principle of showing preference to Farmer-Labor applicants in the absence of a civil service system and pointed out that Strout had no authority over department heads in hiring and firing. The minority member held that the investigating committee's failure to hear all the witnesses caused it to reach erroneous conclusions on matters pertaining to state purchasing contracts and the so-called private dining room.

The immediate result of the investigation, so far as the Department of Administration and Finance was concerned, was reflected in the laws enacted by the 1935 legislature. Construction of the new $1,200,000 hospital for the insane and of buildings and improvements at existing state institutions for 1935–37 was taken from the Big Three, and the Board of Control was authorized to enter into the necessary contracts for these projects.[52] Operation of the commission's new classification and compensation plan for state employees was suspended, and the department heads were given more independence in fixing salaries.[53] An attempt was made to undermine the budget function by refusing to vote an appropriation for printing the next biennial budget document and by providing only a small appropriation of $1,000 for "printing the biennial summary," a brief digest of current, requested, and recommended appropriations with blank spaces for noting legislative action.[54] The appropriation for operating the Department of Administration and Finance was reduced to $92,000 [55] for the next two years. This amount is to be compared with the $108,000 that had been available in the previous two years and the still larger sums that had been appropriated before 1933.

commission. If this is not done and the proposed bill [to require advertising for bids for purchases] is not enacted into law, the 'Big Three' should be abolished, some responsible Finance Division should be established in its place, headed by one responsible, experienced person, answerable to the appointive officer, and subject to removal for cause" (*ibid.*, p. 55).

[51] *Report of Investigating Committee* [minority report], p. 3.

[52] *Session Laws*, 1935, Ch. 383. Under the terms of the 1925 reorganization act the Commission of Administration and Finance had been responsible for negotiating building construction contracts, except for the State Office Building. See above, page 29.

[53] *Session Laws*, 1935, Ch. 391, Sec. 37.

[54] *Ibid.*, Sec. 17, item 4.

[55] *Ibid.*, items 1 and 2.

New Commission Members and Governors

In the fall of 1935 Strout was replaced as budget commissioner and director of personnel by the appointment of Paul A. Rasmussen, dean of men at Concordia College, Moorhead, Minnesota. In May 1936 Erickson announced his resignation as purchasing commissioner and Philip Sundby, an assistant in the purchasing office for five years, was elevated to commission membership.

The change in the budget and personnel position was followed during the next year by the introduction of new policies. Less emphasis was subsequently given to Farmer-Labor party indorsement for all state jobs, though the handling of patronage remained on a political basis. More significant, however, in terms of the purposes of the Big Three, were the changes Rasmussen introduced in the budget and accounting division. Preparation of complete state budgets, tightening-up of the process of expenditure control, utilization of field visits to assist in budget problems, and improvements in the budgetary accounting structure were some of the evidences of the new business policies.

Governor Olson's health was failing, and he died in the summer of 1936. Lieutenant Governor Hjalmar Petersen, Askov newspaper editor and publisher, succeeded to the position of chief executive. Petersen had already been nominated to run for a position on the Railroad and Warehouse Commission. In a state-wide radio address a few days after taking office Governor Petersen pledged himself to carry on Governor Olson's principles and to conduct the business of government with honesty, efficiency, and sincerity of purpose. He asserted that expenditures would be watched closely, that efforts would be made to get the largest service possible out of each dollar spent, and that a plan then being prepared by the Big Three would offer a chance to save the state a million dollars a year.[56] A civil service law to assure the competency of state employees and to create a career service in the state government was recommended.

[56] "At present the Commission of Administration and Finance is preparing some very definite recommendations looking to the introduction of more business efficiency in state government. These recommendations cover certain practices which will require statutory enactment to correct, and they will be presented to the public and the Legislature with the budget next January. They will call for such improvements as the combination of certain administrative units, the rearrangement of the financial system, and a definite program of planning for the state government. These recommendations, if adopted, will save the state well over a million dollars a year" (address of Governor Hjalmar Petersen, quoted in full in the *St. Paul Pioneer Press*, August 29, 1936).

COMMISSION OF ADMINISTRATION AND FINANCE

Elmer Benson, whom Olson had appointed to fill a vacancy in the United States Senate a year earlier, was the Farmer-Labor nominee for governor in 1936. Campaigning principally on pledges to "carry on" for the late Governor Olson, Farmer-Laborites enjoyed their greatest victory at the polls, electing not only the governor and United States Senator, but also filling every state elective office on the party ballot except secretary of state.[57] In the legislature the victorious party was able to organize the House of Representatives, but the Senate, which held over from the 1934 election, continued to be dominated by the conservatives.

In the fall of 1936 Commissioner Rasmussen drew widespread editorial commendation for a series of press releases setting forth the state's budget problems and the necessity for reductions in expense and promising recommendations in the 1937 budget document for a balanced budget, a civil service plan, and some administrative reorganizations.[58] When the printed budget appeared, it contained comparatively conservative recommendations for appropriations, a plan for a pay-as-you-go basis of state financing, and a proposed allocation of funds for a civil service department. Gone were the expected suggestions for administrative consolidations,[59] and present were several references to Governor-elect Benson's tax program. It was soon apparent, however, that the budget document did not really represent the governor's views.

The governor's inaugural message recommended the appropriation of many millions in excess of the budget that went to the legislature. Benson desired these increased expenditures in order to provide funds for the state to assume the counties' share of old age assistance; for various educational purposes—the payment of educational aids in full, new liberal grants to provide free transportation for pupils all over the state, an enlarged program of health education, and an adult education program; for the administration of a Minnesota Youth Act, for which the sponsors wanted a million dollars as a starter; and for many other purposes not mentioned in the budget requests or recommendations.[60] A few days after

[57] The Republicans also held on to the position of state auditor, whose four-year term did not expire then.

[58] At the same time the metropolitan newspapers were opposing Governor-elect Benson. Significantly, a few days after they began to praise Rasmussen, the budget office suddenly stopped issuing the press releases.

[59] The governor's inaugural message contained suggestions along this line.

[60] He recommended, for example, a state advisory power commission, a state planning board, and a state agency to collect unpaid wages, together with appropria-

his inauguration the governor advanced a recommendation for a $17,000,000 relief program; a maximum of $11,000,000 had been recommended in the budget. Disputes over expenditures and tax measures were not settled in the ninety days allotted to the legislature, and a special session was necessary shortly after the close of the regular session. When the special session was adjourned, revenue fund appropriations were far in excess of anticipated receipts for the second year of the biennium, 1938–39. The tumultuous 1937 sessions had done the biggest job of budget unbalancing in the state's history.

Recommended Changes

The year 1937 saw recommendations for changes in the state's financial administration advanced from three different sources. At the beginning of the regular legislative session a joint Interim Tax Committee of the legislature made a lengthy report. Simultaneously, the biennial budget recommendations, prepared by Commissioner Rasmussen, appeared. In the fall the report of the Minnesota State Finance and Tax Survey, prepared under the direction of Harry Fiterman, was made public.

Tackling the problems from different viewpoints and with varying political backgrounds, the three sets of recommendations arrived at very similar conclusions. The Interim Tax Committee, which was controlled by conservatives, was concerned primarily with a study of the existing tax structure, but it found that an intelligent study of the tax problem required some attention to problems of governmental expenditure, the possibility of more effective financial administration, and opportunities for economy. The recommendations of the budget commissioner, a Farmer-Labor official, were based primarily upon a study of finances and administrative problems from the operating point of view. The Fiterman survey, presumably free from political influence, was made through a grant of federal emergency funds and was concerned with the whole future development of Minnesota's government and industry.

In its study of budget and fiscal control the Interim Tax Committee pointed out a series of weaknesses in existing practices — failure of governors to assume budget leadership, incompleteness of

tions to finance them; five new state radio stations for criminal apprehension work; appropriations for a consumers' research bureau; moneys for a larger conservation research program.

budget documents up through 1935, failure to use the allotment system as a positive factor for economy and efficiency, lack of modern accounting and financial reporting methods, and various difficulties caused by the use of special funds, continuing appropriations, and failure to lapse unused appropriation balances. The committee also criticized the "spoils system" of handling personnel and deplored the lack of completely centralized purchasing.[61]

The Fiterman report criticized the large number of dedicated funds, continuing appropriations, inadequate handling of receipts, and inadequate accounting. The report praised the Department of Administration and Finance as "a very useful adjunct to state administration," but pointed out that it was weak since its control had never been entirely centralized or complete. Exemption of certain departments from the operation of the allotment system and from centralized purchasing was criticized.[62]

The Interim Tax Committee, the Rasmussen budget, and the Fiterman report all made similar suggestions and recommendations with respect to a number of points:

1. The allotment system should be strengthened by making all expenditures of the state so far as possible subject to quarterly budget control.

2. Provision should be made for centralizing all state purchasing.

3. Recruitment of personnel should be removed from the Department of Administration and Finance.[63]

4. Specially dedicated funds and continuing appropriations of receipts and balances should be discontinued, with the exception of the few funds created by the constitution. The three reports agreed that all other money should be placed in the general fund of the state and that departments should secure authorization to spend money only through direct appropriations by the legislature.

5. Accounting practices should be strengthened. The Interim Tax

[61] *Report of the Legislative Tax Commission of Investigation and Inquiry,* 1937. See pp. 72–75, 102, 128–36.
[62] "Report of the Minnesota State Finance and Tax Survey," *St. Paul Dispatch,* November 18, 1937, and following issues.
[63] Rasmussen recommended the creation of a separate department of civil service; Fiterman recommended removing personnel functions from the Big Three and the adoption of a merit system, inferring that a separate department of civil service should be created; while the Interim Tax Committee called for the creation of a merit system to be administered by a personnel agency, which would be placed in the central finance department but would be controlled by a nonpolitical three-member civil service commission.

Committee recommended the adoption of accounting practices that would make possible timely and effective reports following standard functional classifications. The Rasmussen budget suggested consideration of the adoption of an accrual accounting system. The Fiterman report agreed.

The Interim Tax Committee also suggested changes in the administrative structure. It proposed that the Commission of Administration and Finance be reorganized by the substitution of a single commissioner appointed by the governor and holding office for an indefinite term, who would prepare the budget for the governor, keep all the accounting records of the state, and operate a quarterly allotment system. He also would be responsible for a completely centralized purchasing system, for the engineering and architectural services, and for the operation and maintenance of the capitol and the office annex building. They suggested that the Minnesota Tax Commission take over the comptroller's auditing duties pertaining to local units of government and that the state auditor, who would lose all accounting and pre-auditing duties under this plan, take over the postauditing duties relating to the state.

The Fiterman report suggested a slightly different arrangement. It too would give the postauditing function to the state auditor and transfer all accounting and pre-auditing duties to the central finance department. It suggested the reorganization of the central finance department under a three-man commission consisting of a budget commissioner in charge of budgeting, accounting, and pre-auditing, a commissioner of purchases responsible for purchasing and printing, and a commissioner of taxation charged with the administrative duties previously exercised by the Minnesota Tax Commission.

No immediate action followed these recommendations. The 1937 legislature was too greatly concerned with revising the tax structure and with battles over the governor's proposed legislation and recommended appropriations. But the Fiterman report, appearing several months after the special session was over, attracted widespread attention.[64] Action on the recommendations was to await the conduct of the next political campaign.

[64] The *St. Paul Dispatch* hailed it as "the most comprehensive survey of Minnesota's governmental problems ever made," and printed the text of the report in serial installments.

COMMISSION OF ADMINISTRATION AND FINANCE

The 1938 Campaign

Even before the 1938 campaign formally opened, events occurred that were to thrust the Commission of Administration and Finance into the fight. On March 11 the State Teachers' College Board addressed a letter to the budget commissioner in which it raised the issue as to whether there was "reckless waste or incompetence" in a building project at Bemidji Teachers' College. Rasmussen attempted to defend the purchasing commissioner, under whose direction the project was being handled, and the subject became a public issue.

The authorization and appropriation for the project had been made by the 1937 legislature,[65] and the commission had hired an architect to design a building. In order to build a larger unit than would be possible within the state appropriation alone, an agreement was made to handle a considerable part of the construction through a federal WPA project. It was the first and only major construction project that the Big Three undertook on this basis.[66] Poor cost estimates by the architect, difficulties encountered in working with unfamiliar WPA methods and labor, and failure to advertise for bids for the material purchased—all these factors contributed to make the cost far exceed the original estimates.

A committee of the Minnesota Association of Architects conducted an investigation of the matter and made public a scathing preliminary report only three days before the primary election. Pearlove, either in his capacity as comptroller or as chairman of the commission,[67] subpoenaed members of the committee and tried to investigate the work of the investigators. Charges of libel and of official misconduct were exchanged on the radio and in the press. The attorney general surprised the commission by holding that the proper procedure was not used in some of the purchases. A final report was made by the architects' committee a few months later. Charges of incompetence and misconduct were again made in this

[65] *Session Laws*, 1937, Ch. 385, and *Special Session Laws*, 1937, Ch. 62.

[66] Construction was usually done on the basis of contracts, let after advertising for bids. When federal PWA moneys were available, the contract method was still used, but WPA regulations prescribed the force-account method.

[67] The commission had been given the power to subpoena witnesses in connection with its power to investigate the administration and management of state affairs (*Session Laws*, 1925, Ch. 426, Art. III, Sec. 3). The comptroller, who had succeeded to the authority conferred upon the public examiner before 1925, had the power to subpoena witnesses in connection with his postauditing duties (*Mason's Minnesota Statutes*, 1927, Sec. 3283).

report, and again countercharges flew. However, no criminal proceedings were ever brought against either the commission members or any commission employees.

The Big Three itself was not a major issue in the campaign, but the summer-long publicity on the Bemidji project gave the opposition an excellent opportunity to make an issue of alleged waste and extravagance in the Benson administration. During the entire campaign period also, Ray P. Chase, former state auditor, issued a series of widely printed press releases charging the Benson administration with extravagance and incompetence. Rasmussen,[68] who was on the Farmer-Labor ticket with Benson, attempted to refute the charges. This immediately drew down upon the Big Three the incisive criticism of Chase, who charged the Commission of Administration and Finance with responsibility for the alleged extravagance and called for its abolition.[69]

The time was expedient for the "outs" to make a constructive suggestion of what action they would take if they became the "ins." Harold E. Stassen, Republican candidate for governor, seized the opportunity and advocated the abolition of the commission in his keynote address. In place of the old Big Three he suggested a new, much more powerful three-man Department of Finance and Taxation, consisting of a comptroller general "with absolute power to curtail unnecessary state expenditures, and municipal expenditures whenever the state is requested to assist in the financing of some municipal project," a commissioner of taxation to replace the Min

[68] Candidate for secretary of state.

[69] In one press release alone (week of May 28, 1938) Chase said:

"The first state department which should be abolished is the Commission of Administration and Finance, of which Mr. Rasmussen is a member. When created it was intended to be a small, compact body to advise the governor. Now it sprawls like a jellyfish over everything without much knowledge of anything. Every argument which impelled the legislature of 1925 to create the 'Big Three' now applies with equal force to its abolition. It was intended to reduce departments and cut costs. Under it departments have increased and costs have increased. It occupies more than 6,000 square feet of capitol floor space and in seven years has cost the taxpayers more than one and a third million dollars. The governor can be given a budget secretary, the auditor the power of pre-audit and the duties of public examiner, the board of control the work of purchasing agent. This is no time for super-boards and duplication of work.

"Of superfluous employees the 'Big Three' are good examples.

"Since the state auditor and treasurer are both constitutional officers and therefore permanent, E. J. Pearlove, comptroller, is as unnecessary as he is expensive.

"The increase of nearly 6,000 in the state payroll is sufficient commentary on the effectiveness of Mr. Rasmussen's work. He can be spared.

"Phil Sundby's record on the Bemidji State Teachers' College building indicates that the present commissioner of purchases can be dismissed without loss to the state. . . ."

45

nesota Tax Commission, and a commissioner of purchases with "the responsibility of making all the purchases for the state." [70]

The Stassen-Benson campaign centered around a number of issues, of which the charges of extravagance and promises of a businesslike administration were only a part. When the votes were counted in November it was found that the Republican party had regained control of the state government after its eight years in opposition and that its candidate for governor had won the race by a plurality of 291,576 votes.

Five Months under Stassen

A complete change took place in the membership of the commission on January 3, 1939, the day that Stassen became governor. Joseph T. Langlais, who had been employed in the public examining division since 1921, became comptroller. Miles Cooper left a position as purchasing agent for Northwest Airlines to become purchasing commissioner. Ralph Jerome, who had been one of the earliest and strongest supporters of the Stassen-for-governor movement, was appointed budget commissioner and was designated director of personnel. The executive secretary, state expert printer, and employment officer were immediately replaced by the new administration. Most of the other employees were released during the succeeding weeks and months and their positions filled with new appointees.

New commission members set to work at once along lines dictated by administration policy. Langlais reorganized the public examining staff and instituted a number of audits of state officials and departments that were coming under gubernatorial and legislative scrutiny. Cooper tightened up the purchasing procedures and began preparations for the centralization of all state buying, which was to come a few months later. Jerome tackled the personnel problem, which was particularly acute because of the pressure for removal of old employees and the appointment of Stassen political supporters before a civil service bill could be enacted and made effective.

Shortly after the election Commissioner Rasmussen had forwarded to the governor-elect copies of all the detailed biennial

[70] Keynote address of Harold E. Stassen, in the 1938 campaign for governor. On advocating centralization of all state purchasing, he pointed out that "at the present time the Department of Administration and Finance makes the purchases for about 30% of the state's requirements."

budget information and requests that the various departments had submitted to the Big Three. A few weeks later a duplicate of Rasmussen's budget recommendations went to the new governor. Stassen requested and secured the assistance of the Minnesota Institute of Governmental Research staff in the preparation of his own recommendations.[71] Every state institution and department was visited either by Stassen or by members of the institute staff. Meanwhile, printing of the regular biennial budget document was held up for ten days in December awaiting word as to the governor's recommendations. The governor was not ready, so the budget was printed with only Rasmussen's recommendations, and in that form it was laid on legislative desks the first week of January. Stassen finished his recommendations in January, and on February 1 he appeared before the legislature personally to present his budget message and a brief four-page printed document containing lump sum recommendations for appropriations and revenue fund income.[72]

Four investigations of the preceding administration were launched in the first months of Stassen's term: one by the Ramsey County attorney and grand jury, a second by the attorney general's office, a third in the form of audits by the new comptroller, and a fourth by a joint legislative investigating committee. The inquiries found two irregularities with respect to the Department of Administration and Finance. The investigations disclosed favoritism and numerous errors in the printing division, and recovery for overpayments to certain printing firms was obtained either through voluntary repayment or by civil action.[73] The other irregularity relating to the Big Three brought an indictment of Joseph Johnson, former employment officer, who was charged with

[71] *Budget Message of Harold E. Stassen*, February 1, 1939, third paragraph.
[72] Comparisons between the Rasmussen and Stassen budgets are difficult to draw because of differences in the treatment of certain items, but excluding relief, for which Rasmussen recommended $10,900,000 for the biennium but for which there was no provision in the Stassen budget, and deducting the amounts recommended in the Stassen budget from dedicated funds that were not budgeted by Rasmussen, the totals are as follows: Rasmussen, $77,171,963.99; Stassen, $76,517,423.00. There were, however, marked differences in the amounts recommended for particular departments and activities.
[73] *Report from the Joint Senate and House Investigating Committee Covering the Acts and Activities of the Various Governmental Departments and Agencies of the State of Minnesota (1939–1940 Interim)*. See pp. 10–12 for material on state printing. An earlier report bears the same title, except that after the word *Minnesota* are the words *1939 Legislative Session*. The earlier one was made to the 1939 session, the other to the 1941 session of the legislature.

removal of certain employment application files; the case never came to trial, however.

Reorganization of the state administration and creation of a civil service department had been among the Stassen campaign promises; disclosures of irregularities under the previous administration made strengthening of the civil administration code an additional piece of "must legislation." The exact form of reorganization, however, remained in doubt until some time after the session opened.[74] Then the governor's proposal for the reorganization as it related to administration and finance emerged. A single commissioner of administration was to be responsible for budgeting, expenditure control, accounting, pre-auditing, purchasing, printing, and property control, while the state auditor, who would thus lose his accounting and pre-auditing powers, would take over the post-auditing function. The proposal met opposition on two counts: the transfer of the auditor's accounting and pre-audit duties to the new department and the creation of a powerful single-headed department instead of a board. It was opposed, as was the reorganization plan of 1925, by a group of senators, who were joined this time by some House leaders friendly to the auditor.

The inevitable compromise followed. By it the auditor retained his duties of keeping the proprietary accounts and doing pre-auditing and gained the responsibility for budgetary accounting and supervision of state accounting. The office of public examiner was re-created to fulfill the postaudit function. The commissioner of administration was given the duties of budgeting, expenditure control, purchasing, printing, and property control.[75] On March 10 a

[74] The evolution of the new organization plan may be traced somewhat as follows: In the campaign of 1938, Stassen had proposed replacing the three-man Commission of Administration and Finance with a new three-man Commission of Finance and Taxation — comptroller general, commissioner of taxation, and commissioner of purchases. In his inaugural address on January 3, 1939, the governor declared that the comptroller's office should be divorced from the so-called Big Three. He suggested that the comptroller be given powers of pre-auditing, expenditure control, budget-making, and accounting installations; and that the office of commissioner of purchases be continued and extended under the administrative branch of the government. Mention is again made, however, of a proposed "department of taxation and finance." But in his budget message on February 1, 1939, the governor made a new suggestion — to replace the Big Three with a "single commissioner of administration and accounting." He again mentioned a "department of taxation and finance," apparently referring only to revenue assessment and collection.

[75] To avoid giving too much power to a single headed department a five-man legislative emergency committee was created and given certain supervisory powers over some of the actions of the commissioner of administration. The new committee was also given the responsibility for allotting relief funds and supervising the administration of them.

48

bill was introduced incorporating the compromise, together with a reorganization of several other departments and specific provisions regulating bidding procedure, requiring budget-balancing, and providing other restrictions on the manner of conducting the state's business. It passed the House on April 17, the Senate on April 19, and was signed by the governor on April 22.[76] At the same time a bill providing for a personnel system based on merit and creating a Department of Civil Service obtained legislative approval and was signed by the governor the same day.[77]

But while the legislature was enacting these measures and other bills in the administration program, it failed to watch the budget-balancing problem. Thus when the session was over the appropriations had exceeded the estimated income provided to meet them. While the governor was deciding upon his choice for the new post of commissioner of administration, it became the duty of the out-going budget commissioner to announce to the departments the excess of appropriations over revenues.[78]

A little more than a week later the governor announced that Leslie M. Gravlin, assistant director of the Minnesota Institute of Governmental Research, would be the new commissioner of administration. On June 6, 1939, Gravlin took the oath of office and the Commission of Administration and Finance passed quietly out of existence.

[76] *Session Laws*, 1939, Ch. 431. The act abolished the Board of Control (in charge of state institutions and public assistance) and created a loosely knit Department of Social Security in charge of a board of three substantially independent directors — social welfare, institutions, and employment security. The former three-member Minnesota Tax Commission was replaced by a single-headed Department of Taxation, but an independent Board of Tax Appeals was established to exercise quasi-judicial powers in tax matters.

[77] *Ibid.*, Ch. 441.

[78] On May 17 the budget commissioner issued forms and instructions for departments to follow in making allotment requests of the new commissioner and indicated that a 10 per cent reserve would be necessary because of the inadequacy of income to finance appropriations.

Chapter 3

COMMISSION PERSONNEL, ORGANIZATION,
AND PROCEDURE

THE background, education, and experience of the twelve people who served on the Commission of Administration and Finance undoubtedly had an influence upon its development and functioning.[1] A study of the organization and procedures used by the commission is also an important preliminary to the study of the department's actual operation. In this phase of the study several significant facts appear: (1) A majority of the commission members were reasonably well fitted for their positions; (2) there was a lack of coordination among the various divisions within the department; (3) the commission tended to grow away from its original character as a deliberative body; and (4) the commission experienced a shift from a generous appropriation in the first half of its history to a pitifully inadequate appropriation in later years.

The Three Comptrollers

There are several striking parallels in the background of the three men who served as state comptrollers and chairmen of the commission. All three had had long experience in government service before they were appointed, all three were well acquainted with accounting and auditing responsibilities, and two of the three were also attorneys.

Henry Rines, who served as comptroller from July 1, 1925, to January 31, 1931, brought to his position considerable experience in public affairs and particularly in public finance. Fifty-three years of age when he was appointed, Rines's public service dated back to the time when he was elected county auditor of Kanabec County at the age of twenty-two. He served ten years as a county auditor, eight years as a member of the state House of Representatives, including one term as speaker, and he had spent eight and a half years as state treasurer when in June 1925 Governor Christianson

---

[1] Information on commission personnel was obtained from editions of the *Legislative Manual of Minnesota*, from newspaper accounts at the time of the commissioners' appointments, and from personal interviews with some of the commission members.

persuaded him to leave that post to become head of the new Department of Administration and Finance at no increase in salary.

Edward J. Pearlove, appointed by Governor Olson February 1, 1931, also took the position of comptroller at no increase over his previous salary. He attended the University of Minnesota and was graduated from the George Washington University law course. He was a member of the bar in both the District of Columbia and the state of Minnesota. Employed by the United States Department of the Treasury shortly after the end of the World War, he earned a series of promotions that raised him to the position of a senior conferee in the Minnesota office of the Bureau of Internal Revenue. Only thirty-six years of age when he became comptroller, Pearlove had the longest period of service of any member of the commission, holding office until January 1939.

Joseph T. Langlais, Governor Stassen's appointee, came out of the ranks of state employees to take office January 3, 1939. A graduate of the Minnesota College of Law and a member of the Minnesota bar since 1919, Langlais was employed as examiner and as supervising examiner in the office of the public examiner and in the Department of Administration and Finance from June 1921 until his appointment as comptroller. He has continued in the position of public examiner since the Commission of Administration and Finance was abolished.

Five Budget Commissioners

Albert J. Peterson, who served as budget commissioner from July 1, 1925, to March 15, 1931, was generally regarded as the personal choice of the governor, who selected him, it was said, because of long acquaintance and confidence in his ability and integrity. Peterson, who was fifty-six years old at the time of his appointment, had been in the banking business about thirty-five years. He had preceded Governor Christianson as representative from Lac qui Parle County in the legislature, where he served in both the 1911 and 1913 sessions. In the latter session (when Henry Rines was speaker of the House) Peterson was chairman of the Committee on Education. In both sessions he was on the Appropriations Committee.

Mrs. Jean W. Wittich, Governor Olson's first appointee as budget commissioner, held B.A. and M.A. degrees and was a member of Phi Beta Kappa, honorary scholastic fraternity. She was graduated from Gettysburg College with majors in economics and mathematics. Her experience included a period as teacher of mathematics and English and some work in statistics and accounting. Chairman of the Department of Efficiency in Government of the Minnesota League of Women Voters and a supporter of the reorganization movement before 1925, Mrs. Wittich had been chairman of Olson's all-party campaign committee in 1930. Mrs. Wittich served from March 16, 1931, to May 15, 1933, when she resigned.

I. C. Strout, budget commissioner from May 24, 1933, to September 30, 1935, was forty years of age when appointed. He had been a railroad official and had had some experience in accounting and auditing. An officer of the Farmer-Labor Educational Association, Strout also had been state director of hotel inspection from 1931 to 1933.

Paul A. Rasmussen, appointed by Governor Olson October 1, 1935, was forty years old at the time. He was a graduate of St. Olaf College, and for nearly fifteen years preceding his appointment he had been a member of the faculty of Concordia College at Moorhead, where he was dean of men and where at various times he did personnel work, assisted in the administration of the institution, and taught public speaking. Rasmussen served until January 1939, when he resigned.

Ralph F. Jerome served as budget commissioner from January 3, 1939, until the commission was abolished June 6, 1939. His education was secured at Staples High School and at a school of military aeronautics conducted by the federal government at the University of Illinois. He had had considerable experience in the automobile business. During the years immediately preceding his term as budget commissioner he was employed in connection with the administration of public relief in Minnesota. Jerome had been an organizer in the Stassen campaign. He was forty-four years old at the time of his appointment.

Four Purchasing Commissioners

Herbert W. Austin, who served as purchasing commissioner from July 1, 1925, to September 30, 1931, was a professional buyer. Son of Minnesota's sixth governor, Austin worked three and a half years for the Chicago Great Western Railroad Company, twenty-three years in the purchasing department of the Northern Pacific Railroad Company, and almost nine years as purchasing agent for the city of St. Paul before he was appointed. He was not a candidate for the position and the newspapers of the time made it clear that he was reluctant to take it until Governor Christianson assured him that there would be no politics connected with it. He was fifty-six years of age at the time of his appointment.

Carl R. Erickson was in a sense Governor Olson's personal appointee to the commission. Erickson, who served from October 1, 1931, to June 30, 1936, had had experience in the real-estate business, investments, insurance, building operations, and building management. He returned to Minnesota from California in order to take the position of purchasing commissioner.

G. Philip Sundby was promoted from his position as assistant commissioner to the position of commissioner of purchases October 1, 1936. He had been in the retail mercantile business in Minneapolis for many years preceding his employment by the state in 1931. A graduate of Minneapolis Central High School and a former student at the University of Minnesota, Sundby was forty-one years of age at the time of his appointment. He served until January 1939.

Miles Cooper was appointed by Governor Stassen on January 3, 1939, and continued as head of the purchasing division when the Commission of Administration and Finance was abolished on June 6. A graduate of Macalester College in St. Paul, Cooper had been purchasing agent for Northwest Airlines from 1930 until his appointment to the Big Three at the age of thirty-four.

Commission Meetings

No rules for formal commission meetings were set down in the law. As a result the practice of the commission with respect to meetings went through some changes as the department developed.

The commission held its first informal meeting in the governor's office shortly after the original appointments were made and daily meetings thereafter were forecast.[2] In the first few months meetings apparently were held almost daily in the offices of the Big Three. But as time progressed and the department's business settled down into an established routine, the frequency of meetings diminished and after the first two years meetings occurred only about twice a week. In later years they were sometimes less often. Regular meeting times were not established and frequently there was no advance notice.

[2] *St. Paul Dispatch,* June 20, 1925.

COMMISSION OF ADMINISTRATION AND FINANCE

Subject matter of the meetings also underwent a change. The early meetings were concerned with the entire business of the department, and the meetings offered a chance for coordinating the work of the various divisions. After routine was established the commissioners began to take more and more individual responsibility for details of administration, bringing their actions to the commission meetings only for approval and ratification. Even then, however, the first commission deliberated at length on personnel orders, general rules, and budgets of the departments. In later years these matters too became the province of a single commissioner, subject to formal ratification by the commission. Meetings of the Big Three were reserved for discussion of major policies and the more important contracts, and occasionally for dealing with complaints and grievances on the part of the vendors and departments.

No records of the commission meetings for the first two years are extant. Minutes from June 30, 1927, to the end of the department's existence in 1939 are on file, however, recorded in four bound books.[3] From 1927 to 1931 the minutes read as if the commission met and formally approved all contracts, budget allotments, and similar items. In 1931 a change was made in the writing of the minutes, and for several years thereafter the minutes show the purchasing commissioner approving contracts, the budget commissioner approving allotments, etc.[4] In the last years the minutes again show the commission approving all documents "on recommendation of" single commission members.

All three commission members were usually present, though there are a number of meetings during the years on record when only two were present, and a few meetings when the purchasing commissioner and the executive secretary (who was acting as deputy comptroller) constituted those present at the "meeting."[5] Meetings were customarily attended only by commission members and the executive secretary, except when the subject for discus-

[3] The minutes for July 2, 1927, record that on that day the commission formally approved its orders number 1 to 47 inclusive, which had apparently been issued during the two preceding years.

[4] The following entry by Mrs. Jean Wittich, budget commissioner, explains the change: "The preceding minutes were written according to the form set up originally when all business cleared through Commission meetings. As the work became better defined, each Commissioner assumed responsibility for those practices peculiar to his position. The following minutes and notations represent the actual picture of Commission activities" ("Minutes of the Commission," Book A, p. 422 [April 1931]).

[5] *Ibid.*, Book C, p. 1051 (September 6, 1935).

sion made it desirable for an interested party to be present. Commission minutes, which did not reflect the discussion but only the action taken, were always open to public inspection. Meetings between the commission and the governor were not too frequent, and when held they were informal in nature and no record of them was kept.

Organization of the Department

The basic law prescribed:

The commission shall be organized in three divisions: a comptroller's division in charge of the comptroller; a budget division in charge of the commissioner of the budget; and a purchase division in charge of the commissioner of purchases.[6]

But it also gave the commission duties with respect to personnel, authorized transfer of the central supply room from the Board of Control, and placed the state expert printer in the new Department of Administration and Finance. In actual practice, therefore, six divisions developed: (1) public examining division, (2) budget and accounting division, (3) personnel division, (4) purchasing division, (5) printing division, and (6) stores division.

Lines of authority between four of these divisions and the commission members were fixed and well defined. The public examining division was under the comptroller, the personnel division was under the commissioner who was designated as personnel director,[7] and the purchasing and stores divisions were under the direction of the purchasing commissioner.

Responsibility for budgetary accounting was placed with the comptroller by the reorganization act, while the supervision of the allotment budget procedure was given to the budget commissioner by the first Big Three. Both officials naturally had an interest in the pre-audit of disbursements. It soon became evident that it was most practicable for one staff to exercise the functions of allotment budgeting, budgetary accounting, and pre-audit of disbursements. Accordingly one group of employees carried on the work of the budgeting and accounting division under dual supervision. In the earlier years the comptroller did most of the supervising, while in the latter years of the Big Three the budget commissioner took the primary responsibility. Preparation of the

[6] *Session Laws,* 1925, Ch. 426, Art. III, Sec. 1.
[7] The budget commissioner was designated as director of personnel except during a part of 1931, when the comptroller functioned in that capacity.

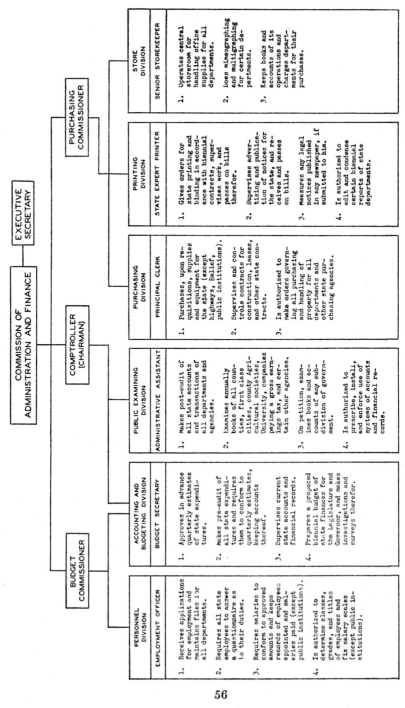

COMMISSION OF
ADMINISTRATION AND FINANCE

EXECUTIVE
SECRETARY

BUDGET
COMMISSIONER

COMPTROLLER
[CHAIRMAN]

PURCHASING
COMMISSIONER

PERSONNEL DIVISION

EMPLOYMENT OFFICER

1. Receives applications for employment and maintains files for all departments.
2. Requires all state employees to answer a questionnaire as to their duties.
3. Requires salaries to conform to approved amounts and keeps records of employees appointed and salaries paid (except public institutions).
4. Is authorized to determine classes, grades, and titles of employees and fix salary scales (except public institutions).

ACCOUNTING AND BUDGETING DIVISION

BUDGET SECRETARY

1. Approves in advance quarterly estimates of state expenditures.
2. Makes pre-audit of all state expenditures and requires them to conform to quarterly estimates, keeping accounts thereof.
3. Supervises current state accounts and financial records.
4. Prepares a proposed biennial budget of state finances for the Legislature and Governor, and makes investigations and surveys therefor.

PUBLIC EXAMINING DIVISION

ADMINISTRATIVE ASSISTANT

1. Makes post-audit of all state accounts and transactions of all departments and agencies.
2. Examines annually books of all counties, first class cities, county Agricultural societies, University, companies paying a gross earnings tax, and certain other agencies.
3. On petition, examines books and accounts of any subdivision of government.
4. Is authorized to prescribe, install, and enforce use of systems of accounts and financial records.

PURCHASING DIVISION

PRINCIPAL CLERK

1. Purchases, upon requisitions, supplies and equipment for the state (except highways, Relief, public institutions).
2. Supervises and controls contracts for construction, leases, and other state contracts.
3. Is authorized to make orders governing and handling all purchasing of property for all departments and other state purchasing agencies.

PRINTING DIVISION

STATE EXPERT PRINTER

1. Gives orders for state printing and binding in accordance with biennial contracts, supervises work, and passes on bills therefor.
2. Supervises advertising and publication of notices for the state, and receives and passes on bills.
3. Measures any legal notices published in any newspaper, if submitted to him.
4. Is authorized to edit and condense certain biennial reports of state departments.

STORE DIVISION

SENIOR STOREKEEPER

1. Operates central storeroom for handling office supplies for all departments.
2. Does mimeographing and multigraphing for certain departments.
3. Keeps books and accounts of its operations and charges departments for their purchases.

Organization of the Minnesota Department of Administration and Finance, created in 1925 (chart prepared by Carl W. Tiller, 1937)

biennial budget was expedited by a group of examiners from the public examining division who worked exclusively under the direction of the budget commissioner for approximately the last four months of each even-numbered year.

The state expert printer, who together with two or three other employees composed the printing division, was responsible to the commission as a whole. Before 1925 the state expert printer had been nominally subject to supervision by a printing commission composed of three elective officials serving ex officio—the auditor, treasurer, and secretary of state.[8] In practice the printing commission appointed the printer, awarded some contracts once a year, and otherwise let the printer function independently. The reorganization act abolished the printing commission and transferred its duties to the Big Three. The printer retained a large degree of independence until 1937, when his offices were consolidated with the rest of the department and his work was somewhat integrated with that of the purchasing division.[9]

Little was done toward coordinating the work of the several divisions. No formal coordination was provided except that which might come out of commission meetings, and most of the time commission meetings were not related to problems of coordination. Some informal coordination did take place, an outstanding example of which was the "pay-roll desk," which served both the personnel division and the budget and accounting division in the pre-audit of payments for personnel services.

The absence of coordination in the organization was constantly revealed in its dealings with other state officials and agencies. Not infrequently the purchasing division made purchases for departments in excess of allotments allowed by the budget division. After the depression set in the personnel division was engaged in creating new places for job-seekers in various departments at the same time that the budget office was trying to hold down budgets and reduce expenditures. The accounting and budgeting division directed departments to keep proper budgetary accounts; however, the public examining division usually confined its postaudit to proprietary accounts, and some departments were thereby led to believe that the keeping of budgetary records was unimportant.

[8] *Mason's Minnesota Statutes*, 1927, Sec. 5671.
[9] From 1925 to 1931 the comptroller and state printer worked together closely; they were personal friends of long standing, and the comptroller was himself a newspaper publisher.

COMMISSION OF ADMINISTRATION AND FINANCE

The stores division expanded its mimeographing and multigraphing services for the departments, while the printing division often encouraged departments to increase their use of its printing facilities.

The Place of the Executive Secretary

The reorganization act authorized the commission to appoint, with the approval of the governor, such employees as would be necessary to carry out the department's responsibilities.[10] The first commission and the governor decided to create the position of executive secretary of the commission, apparently believing that such an officer would be able to coordinate the work of the various divisions within the department.

Ample precedent existed for this move. Not only most of the unpaid state boards, such as the Board of Education, the Board of Health, and the Livestock Sanitary Board, had executive secretaries or executive officers, but each of the major full-time boards then in existence had similar positions. The Board of Control, the Tax Commission, the Industrial Commission, and the Railroad and Warehouse Commission each had an executive secretary, who was to a large degree in charge of the employees and the conduct of work within the department. But in creating the position of executive secretary, the new Commission of Administration and Finance lost sight of a significant difference between itself and the other full-time boards then in existence. In the case of the other boards the members acted primarily as a unit and separate administrative duties were not prescribed for each member by law. In the new Commission of Administration and Finance, however, the responsibility for direct supervision of the various activities had been delegated to specific commission members by law. The act had apparently not contemplated employment of an executive secretary.[11]

Therefore, in reality the position of the executive secretary had very few "executive" duties attached to it. All affairs pertaining to the public examining division were directly under the comptroller; in like manner the employees, activities, and transactions pertain-

---

[10] *Session Laws*, 1925, Ch. 426, Art. III, Sec. 3.

[11] The law did authorize the commission, with the approval of the governor, to appoint assistants or deputies for each member, and this power was exercised in the appointment of a deputy public examiner and an assistant purchasing commissioner.

ing to budgeting and purchasing were responsibilities of the budget commissioner and the purchasing commissioner. The executive secretary was left with such tasks as the supervision of the information clerk, the opening of general mail not addressed to any particular division, the signing of numerous documents, and the recording of minutes of commission meetings. At no time did any of the executive secretaries have a real opportunity to give the position the significance the title implied.

Personality is a determining factor in many organizations. The first executive secretary, Frank Nutter, brought with him to the job a background of engineering and contracting experience; accordingly the commission assigned to him much of the responsibility for the contract work of the department. Succeeding executive secretaries retained this duty, working in cooperation with the purchasing commissioner. Knud Wefald, during his short term, also spent some time interviewing job applicants. J. Earle Lawler, with an advertising and newspaper background, added press relations to the responsibilities at one time attaching to the executive secretary's work, and during a period when there was a vacancy in the state printer's office, he also took charge of the printing division. Richard Golling, an attorney by profession, assisted in personnel work and inquired into the legality of some claims reaching the department for pre-audit, in addition to continuing some supervision of contracts written by the commission.[12]

Appropriations and Staff

It was originally estimated that the Department of Administration and Finance would cost $75,000 a year, in addition to the salaries and expenses of the public examining division and the state printer, which were already supported by existing appropriations in 1925. But the department was one of those rarities in government service whose expenditures at no time come up to the original estimates.

The first commission was economy-minded even toward its own expenses, and it moved cautiously in the organization of the department and in the expansion of its activities. At the end of the first biennium $56,977 of the original $150,000 appropriation was

[12] The years of service of the four executive secretaries were as follows: Nutter, 1925–31; Wefald, 1931–32; Lawler, 1932–39; Golling, 1939.

COMMISSION OF ADMINISTRATION AND FINANCE

carried forward as an undisbursed balance.[13] The legislature reduced the appropriation for the next two years accordingly, but
the end of the second biennium found undisbursed balances of
$57,408 on hand. By this time the commission had found that its
normal expenditures approximated $50,000 a year for salaries and
$5,000 to $10,000 a year for supplies and expense. Separate appropriations were provided for these two items.

After the change from a Republican to a Farmer-Labor administration, the legislature (of which a majority in one house and
sometimes in both were always in the political opposition) became
more and more penurious with the Big Three. The low point in
appropriations was reached when the 1935 legislature gave only
$40,000 a year for salaries and $5,000 and $7,000 respectively for
each year of the next biennium for supplies and expense. During
this time the commission was finding that the law imposed upon
it a number of duties that earlier commission members had not
carried out. The Big Three pleaded for more money to enable it to
carry out the original purposes and responsibilities of the department as expressed in the statutes, but the legislative leaders turned
a deaf ear. The 1937 legislature did raise the total appropriation
to $56,000 for the next year and a somewhat similar amount for
the following year. In 1939, with the Republicans back in control of
the administration and with the department about to be reorganized, the legislature raised the appropriation to $76,500 for the year
ending that June 30.[14] The expenses of the new Department of

[13] They were able to save this amount because there had been no attempt to
consolidate the purchasing staffs of the university or the Highway Department with
the commission's staff; and no expenses had been incurred for some of the other activities that had been contemplated when the reorganization act was passed.

[14] The following table reflects the appropriations and disbursements for administrative expense, exclusive of the public examining division, from 1925 to 1939. Refunds
(totaling $2,502.74) have been deducted from disbursements.

Fiscal Year	Balance Forward Start of Year	Direct Appropria- tions	Disbursements		Balance Forward End of Year
			Salaries	Other Expenses	
1925–26 .... {		$75,000.00	$32,859.20	$ 7,695.92	$34,444.88
{	$ 114.84*	6,150.00*	4,400.00*	1,808.52*	56.32*
1926–27 .... {	34,444.88	75,000.00	44,646.57	7,820.93	56,977.38
{	56.32*	6,150.00*	4,395.00*	1,794.19*	17.13*
1927–28	56,994.51	47,900.00	53,549.57	7,538.31	43,806.63

* Separate appropriations for the printing division, 1925–27. The printing of the
biennial budget and the legislative printing were paid for from other appropriations
not shown here. Operation of the store was financed from a separate revolving fund.
Budget examiners were loaned by the public examining division.

60

Administration prior to June 30 were to be paid from any appropriation balance left from the old department.

Separate appropriations for salaries, supplies, and expenses of the public examining division—a custom carried over from the period preceding 1925—were continued throughout the life of the Big Three. The amount of moneys available for this function kept pace with the growing scope of auditing activities. Only once was the appropriation so small that the expenditures practically equaled the total available to spend; on several other occasions, however, the salary appropriation was exhausted, whereas a balance remained in the supplies and expense account. Before 1931 the cost of county audits was met by direct appropriations from the state treasury, while audits of other civil subdivisions were made on a reimbursement basis; since then counties have been required to pay the state for the audits.[15] This change had the effect of reducing direct appropriations and increasing reappropriated receipts of the public examining divison.[16]

Note 14. Continued

Fiscal Year	Balance Forward Start of Year	Direct Appropriations	Disbursements		Balance Forward End of Year
			Salaries	Other Expenses	
1928–29	43,806.63	74,400.00	50,070.06	10,728.13	57,408.44
1929–30	57,408.44	40,000.00	50,520.81	5,374.49	41,513.14
1930–31	41,513.14	50,000.00	50,234.11	10,016.23	31,262.80
1931–32	31,262.80	40,000.00	48,971.90	6,438.23	15,852.67
1932–33	15,852.67	50,000.00	49,846.50	9,830.13	6,176.04
1933–34	6,176.04	47,000.00	44,563.28	8,117.65	495.11
1934–35	495.11	55,000.00	45,463.45	9,868.03	163.63
1935–36	163.63	45,000.00	39,968.41	5,013.22	182.00
1936–37	182.00	47,000.00	40,012.56	7,123.55	45.89
1937–38	45.89	56,000.00	49,934.45	6,014.16	97.28
1938–39	97.28	76,500.00	61,255.76	5,853.51	8,488.01

[15] *Session Laws*, 1931, Chs. 125, 246. In 1929 the rates to be charged the subdivisions by the public examiner had been increased, a change which also increased the division's reappropriated receipts.

[16] The following table reflects the direct appropriations, totals available for expenditure, and disbursements of the public examining division from 1925 to 1939.

Fiscal Year	Direct Appropriations	Total Available*	Disbursements		Balance Carried Forward
			Salaries	Expenses	
1925–26	....$69,550.00	$ 83,121.53	$ 60,900.33	$17,605.42	$ 4,615.78
1926–27	.... 69,550.00	82,518.33	47,584.94	27,426.78	7,506.61
1927–28	.... 68,000.00	88,574.63	59,023.20	17,417.92	12,133.51
1928–29	.... 68,000.00	99,190.51	63,070.75	18,473.92	17,645.84
1929–30	.... 60,000.00	101,679.71	76,284.25	20,139.90	5,255.56
1930–31	.... 86,750.00	113,377.61	84,439.80	27,858.48	1,079.33

* These figures are the sum of direct appropriations, balance carried forward, and reappropriated receipts.

COMMISSION OF ADMINISTRATION AND FINANCE

All the expenses of the Big Three were not met from appropriations to the commission. Salaries and expenses of the purchasing agents for the Highway Department, for the Board of Control, and for the State Relief Agency were always paid from appropriations to the several departments named, even when that purchasing was under the supervision of the purchasing commissioner. During the later years, when the appropriations were drastically curtailed, employees were shifted on various occasions and for varying periods of time to other pay rolls. Some nonstore employees were temporarily shifted to the store revolving fund, some accounting division employees were placed on the public examining division pay roll, and other Big Three employees were at times paid directly from Highway Department and State Relief Agency moneys.[17] No record of the amounts so paid exists.

The permanent staff of the department remained relatively constant in size throughout the entire period. The full-time employees in the several divisions other than the examining division numbered between twenty and twenty-five, while the latter division increased from thirty to forty-five during the years 1925 to 1932 and then remained at about the last figure. Temporary help also showed little fluctuation except in 1937–38 and again in 1939. Position titles in 1938 included the following: executive secretary, state printer, assistant purchasing commissioner, employment officer and assistant employment officer, administrative assistant, budget secretary, accountant, auditor, examiner, senior storekeeper, stenographer, and clerk.

Note 16. Continued

Fiscal Year	Direct Appropriations	Total Available*	Disbursements		Balance Carried Forward
			Salaries	Expenses	
1931–32	.... 93,000.00	148,119.08	101,296.19	29,552.55	16,933.60
1932–33	.... 93,000.00	179,330.33	107,853.41	33,404.67	38,072.25
1933–34	.... 65,000.00	175,311.14	95,406.63	23,887.36	56,017.15
1934–35	.... 75,000.00	198,788.97	99,761.03	27,785.26	71,242.68
1935–36	.... 30,000.00	170,600.57	102,582.72	31,017.27	37,000.58
1936–37	.... 55,000.00	165,199.77	109,494.44	29,374.98	26,330.35
1937–38	.... 48,000.00	156,864.09	112,877.73	31,335.84	12,650.52
1938–39	.... 58,000.00	138,460.89	99,404.20†	26,443.17	12,613.52

* These figures are the sum of direct appropriations, balance carried forward, and reappropriated receipts.

† In the latter part of 1938–39 some of the examiners' salaries were paid directly from a special appropriation for the general investigation of state departments.

[17] This fact was noted in the 1935 investigation report, in the 1937 budget document (p. 95), in mimeographed material submitted by the department to the 1937 legislature, and in the 1939 budget document (p. 64).

Chapter 4

BUDGETING

ONE of the features of the reorganization plan was the creation of a budget agency that would enable the chief executive to present a complete, unified financial plan biennially for the consideration of the legislature. In practice, however, the original plan for an executive-type budget was ineffective in that: (1) most of the budgets submitted to the legislature were in no sense complete financial programs; (2) the budgets sometimes reflected the governor's financial views incompletely or incorrectly and they were not usually regarded as being the governor's budget; and (3) the legislature as a whole never utilized the biennial budget in the way that had been contemplated. These developments are reviewed in the following examination of the budget process.

Plans for an Executive Budget

The reorganization act provided that all departments, officials, and agencies of the government should file budget estimates with the Commission of Administration and Finance on or before September 1 of each year preceding the convening of the legislature.[1] The commissioner of the budget was charged with the responsibility of investigating, approving, disapproving, and altering departmental estimates, subject to review and revision by the Big Three as a whole. Not later than December 1 the recommendations of the budget commissioner and the Big Three were to be transmitted to the governor and the governor-elect.[2] Shortly after his inauguration the governor was required to submit to the legislature a budget embracing "the amounts in detail recommended by him" for all appropriations, estimated revenues from all recommended sources of revenue, and his recommendations for borrowings, if any.

The budget was to be a complete financial plan in all respects. It was made mandatory for "every department, official, and agency of the state" to file budget estimates "for all receipts and expenditures."[3] The printed budget itself was to cover "all receipts and

---

[1] *Session Laws,* 1925, Ch. 426, Art. III, Sec. 9.

[2] The term of the governor in Minnesota is two years.

[3] Apparently the all-inclusive language of this portion of the 1925 act was never questioned except in the case of the university. In March 1930, upon request of

63

expenditures of the state government" according to the law. Major divisions of the budget were set forth by statute.

The governor's responsibility for the finished budget was made exceptionally clear by the reorganization act. The act provided not only that the governor should transmit the budget to the legislature, but also that the budget should "include in detail definite recommendations of the Governor relative to the amounts which should be appropriated" for the various items, and that it should also "include definite recommendations of the governor for financing the expenditures recommended, and the relative amounts to be raised from ordinary revenue, direct taxes, or loans."

It was provided that in the preparation of the budget the books, records, accounts, resources, and full cooperation of the comptroller's division should be available to the budget commissioner, and that the governor might call upon the comptroller for information and assistance in the preparation and review of the budget.

Preparation of the Budget

Staff assistance in the preparation of the budget was never great. In the early and later years of the commission the budget commissioner was provided with a permanent employee who could give at least part of his time the year around to work related to the preparation of the biennial budget. In the middle years of the commission's history, even this assistance was not forthcoming. The actual detailed work of handling the budget estimates was done by a small group of men borrowed from the public examining division for a period of three to four months out of each biennium, together with some assistance from the personnel division on matters of salaries and some assistance from employees engaged in the day-to-day operations of budgetary accounting and pre-auditing disbursements.

Blank forms for departments to use in making their budget estimates and requests were provided by the Big Three. During the first ten years large oversized forms were used; these represented modifications and revisions of the blanks in use during the decade preceding 1925. In 1936 a complete change was made in the forms, and letter-size blanks were provided. Some further revision of the forms came in 1938, when legal-size blanks were used. In the prep-

A. J. Peterson, budget commissioner, Attorney General Benson held informally that the university did come under the budget-making authority of the Big Three.

aration of the last two budgets department requests were filed in duplicate so that one copy could be preserved intact for the legislature; before that time, when the large handwritten forms were used, only one copy of the request was required. Instructions for submission of estimates in 1936 and 1938 called for additional information with respect to departmental duties, work programs, and accomplishments.[4]

Budget hearings and individual conferences with department heads always characterized the preparation of the budget.[5] The first commission pursued the practice of visiting state institutions as a body in order to go over their budget requests, and the commission as a whole held budget conferences with the heads of the state departments that requested the larger appropriations. Later commissions left these duties almost exclusively to the budget commissioner. Departments that operated on reappropriated receipts (dedicated revenues), including Highways and Rural Credits, were not summoned for budget discussions, however. Public hearings were not the practice when the budget was being prepared but were reserved for the use of the legislature after the budget was presented to it.[6]

Because the three commission members worked together in the preparation of the first three budgets, there was no question as to the commission's approval of the budget commissioner's work. When the 1933 budget was prepared, however, the budget commissioner presented her finished work to the Big Three for its formal approval and the other two commissioners refused to concur in her recommendations. They wrote a letter to the governor in which they expressed disagreement with the budget and recommended concurrence in the requests of the Board of Control for building construction at the state institutions, which had been disapproved by

[4] See instruction booklet for 1936 (mimeographed), p. 4, and instruction booklet for 1938 (mimeographed), p. 4.

[5] Mrs. Wittich was the first budget commissioner to assemble department heads and finance officers together for a general budget conference. Two hundred and thirty persons, including eighty guests, were present at this conference held on November 24, 1931. Governor Olson and Professor Morris B. Lambie of the University of Minnesota addressed the conference on budget problems and procedures.

[6] Since even the legislative hearings were usually attended only by supporters of proposed appropriations, there is little likelihood that "public" hearings by the commission would have attracted others than department heads and perhaps an occasional newspaper reporter. Public interest in budget preparation was never high, except perhaps in the fall of 1936, when Commissioner Rasmussen aroused considerable interest with a series of press releases on the budget problem.

the budget commissioner. In the preparation of later budgets commission approval of the budget commissioner's recommendations was not an issue.

A handicap in the preparation of the budget was the tardiness with which department heads submitted their estimates and requests. Although the requests were all due on September 1, the majority of them did not reach the Big Three until about October 1, and often some of the major departments failed to present their budgets until several weeks later. The governor was either unconcerned or else unable to secure better cooperation from departments on this point. The 1927 budget called attention to the difficulties encountered as a result of the dilatory practices of departments but expressed the opinion that greater familiarity with the budget process would cause departments to get their requests in on time.

The Budget Document

Seven budgets were published by the Commission of Administration and Finance.[7] Most of them were voluminous in make-up. The first three were approximately ten by fourteen inches in size, with 220, 324, and 370 pages, respectively. The 1933 budget, the only one to be mimeographed instead of printed, had a page size of nine by twelve inches and was two and one-half inches in thickness.[8] In 1935 the budget was nine and a half by eleven and a half inches and totaled 533 pages. The 1937 and 1939 documents were seven and a half by eleven inches in page size and contained 492 and 475 pages, respectively.

Completeness in the budget document was achieved only sporadically. Rarely did the budget actually present a well-rounded fiscal plan for the state. The first budget was restricted primarily to activities supported by direct appropriations. Later, attempts were made to present data on trunk highways, rural credits, game and fish, and other funds and activities that operated on reappropriated receipts. Only the budgets of 1933, 1937, and 1939, however, presented the complete picture of all the funds, receipts, and disbursements that were involved in state fiscal operations. The requirement that the budget show the sources of income necessary

[7] The four-page budget summary that Governor Stassen submitted to the legislature in 1939 is not included in this discussion of the budget documents. It was not intended to fulfill the same function as a regular budget document.

[8] The highest page number is 1219, but page numbers were not consecutive, so that the book probably was about 900 pages.

to finance recommended appropriations was not met in four out
of seven occasions. Means of financing the proposed expenditures
were set forth only in the 1933, 1937, and 1939 documents. The
1927 budget explained the attitude of the budget commissioner at
other times:

Section 9 of the Reorganization Act requires that recommendations be
made to the governor for financing the recommended appropriations. It
would appear to be more practical to make such recommendations after the
approximate amount to be appropriated by the Legislature has been ascertained with reasonable certainty and that course will be followed unless an
estimate of the required tax levy for State Revenue purposes is requested
prior to such time.[9]

Summaries were often poor, and until 1937 there was little or no
information concerning the department activities to be carried on
with the appropriations. All budgets, however, contained detailed
tables relating to expenditures. The earlier documents detailed expenditures according to a classification of more than seventy items;
gradually, however, the amount of detail was reduced until the
last budget in 1939 showed expenditures within each appropriation according to only five items. The 1933 budget was enlivened
and illustrated by the use of charts, graphs, photographs, quotations, and descriptive matter. The 1939 budget showed a definite
shift from tabular information to the use of reading matter; it
contained explanations of the history and use of each account, the
main elements in the request, and the basis on which the recommendation was determined.

Significant in the budget documents was a method of treating
the recommended appropriations so as to emphasize the budget as
the work of the budget commissioner rather than as the plan of
the governor. From 1927 to 1935 inclusive the detailed recommendations for appropriations and expenditures appeared under the
headings "Recommended by Budget Commissioner" or "Budget
Commissioner's Recommendations." The 1937 and 1939 budgets,
which omitted the departmental requests in the detailed tables,
used the heading "Estimates" over figures for the following bien-
niums, and an explanation in the front of the documents indicated
that they were the recommendations of the budget commissioner. At no time did the tables in the printed budgets indicate

[9] *Biennial Budget*, 1927–29, p. v. The earlier budgets did contain comparative
statements of revenue receipts, including estimates for the ensuing biennial periods.

any disagreement between the budget commissioner and the governor nor any revision by the chief executive of the budget commissioner's recommendations.

Budget Recommendations

Recommendations in the biennial budgets dealt with five general subjects: appropriations, revenues, borrowing, financial administration, and departmental reorganizations.

All seven budgets paid careful attention to the problem of recommended appropriations. Except in 1935 a narrative summary near the front of the budget document attempted to explain the major recommendations; generally the explanations were designed to perform the double task of indicating why certain increases were recommended over the appropriations of the previous session, and yet why the budget commissioner recommended reductions from the original budget requests of the departments. The 1933 budget featured specific comments of the budget commissioner concerning the financial condition of the state and the requests of and recommendations for the principal state agencies.

Two practices that prevailed throughout the entire history of the Big Three militated seriously against the effectiveness of the budget-making process. In the first place, the allocation by constitutional or statutory provisions of the revenues derived from specific taxes or other sources to particular departments or functions resulted practically in removing such expenditures, amounting to as much as 75 to 80 per cent of the total, from effective budgetary and legislative control. Second, since the legislature regularly reappropriated the unused balances of departmental appropriations for preceding years, these balances were reserved to the spending agencies in the budget plan rather than being allocated in terms of future need.[10]

The 1933, 1937, and 1939 budgets, reflecting mounting governmental expenditures and demands for shifting the tax burden, contained definite revenue recommendations.[11] The 1933 budget

---

[10] Cf. *Report of the Legislative Tax Commission of Investigation and Inquiry*, January 4, 1937, pp. 73–74; *An Analysis of Minnesota State Fiscal Operations, 1932–1940* (Minnesota Institute of Governmental Research Bulletin No. 11, Minneapolis, 1940), pp. 26–27; and *Seventh Biennial Budget of Minnesota*, 1939–41, p. 18.

[11] The 1929 and 1931 budgets warned that new sources of revenue or increases in direct tax levies would be required to meet estimated expenditures, but they contained no recommendations on legislative policy in this regard.

suggested such revenue changes as the diversion of the royalty on iron ore from the trust funds to the revenue fund, diversion of highway moneys for oil inspection and gax-tax collection expenses, repeal of the state property-tax levies for roads and for university buildings, and submission of a constitutional amendment to the voters providing a four-year moratorium on all trust-fund accumulations, the trust-fund receipts to be shifted to the revenue fund. The 1937 budget recommended a new source of revenue in terms of additional taxation on the iron ore industry; increases in the rates of inheritance, income, and gasoline taxes; and a reduction of nearly one third in the state property-tax rates. In 1939 the budget commissioner again recommended a severance tax on iron ore, an increase in income taxes, retention of the existing gas-tax rate, and a shift in the use of some revenues. The governor's budget summary in 1939 recommended increases in occupation and royalty taxes on iron ore, an assessment of 5 per cent on dedicated receipts for the benefit of the revenue fund, and a shift in the use of some revenues.

Although the state issued bonds and certificates of indebtedness in every biennium after 1925, only the last two budgets contained complete estimates of future borrowing and forecasts of the outstanding debt at the end of the biennium.[12] The 1935 budget recommended borrowing to finance a general improvement program at state institutions—a new departure in state finance—but it made no reference to relief and other borrowing. The 1937 budget contained an examination of the debt situation and recommended no more borrowing except rural credit amortization certificates. In 1939 both the budget commissioner and the governor recommended new borrowing for relief and a building program.

Earlier budgets contained only a very few recommendations for changes in financial administration—principally, a more simplified appropriation bill and a new method of paying printing bills. The 1933 budget included pertinent observations on a number of fiscal matters, such as dedicated revenues, contingent and revolving funds, departmental accounting, and inventories. The 1937 budget listed ten recommendations for changes in financial procedure, dealing with: (1) the allotment system, (2) types of appro-

---

[12] The earlier budgets, beginning with 1929, merely included summary and detailed tables showing outstanding state obligations (bonds and certificates of indebtedness as of specified dates.

priations, (3) budgeting and reporting receipts, (4) fiscal year of state agencies, (5) transfers of funds, (6) call feature of bonds, (7) a perpetual inventory of property, (8) consolidation of appropriation accounts, (9) accrual accounting, and (10) centralized purchasing. The 1939 budget presented a summary of existing defects in Minnesota's financial management, principles of good financial administration, and recommendations for eight changes—repeating many of the recommendations made two years earlier and adding a suggestion relating to assessment and collection of revenues. Both in 1937 and in 1939 the budget commissioner set forth the existing legal difficulties and hindrances to carrying out all the purposes and ideals of the reorganization act and pleaded for legislative action to make possible desirable changes in fiscal management practices.

Reorganization of state agencies received attention only in the 1939 budget document. In that year Commissioner Rasmussen pointed out the existence of more than one hundred state departments and agencies and suggested some consolidations. He warned, however, that the 1925 reorganization was not completely effective and that future consolidation should involve more than changes in title and name. New departments of Public Welfare, Veterans' Affairs, and Registrations were suggested, and the consolidation of state activities dealing with taxation and agriculture in the existing departments bearing those titles was recommended.[13]

The Governor and the Budget

The extent of the governor's participation in the budget process varied. Governor Christianson made a practice of setting a maximum figure for the revenue fund appropriations beyond which the Big Three was not supposed to go in its budget recommendations. From time to time during the preparation of the first budgets the governor made it a practice to consult with members of the commission, and it is quite probable that he also discussed recommended appropriations with the heads of major state departments individually. Governor Olson took an active interest in the budget-balancing problems that faced Mrs. Wittich in the preparation of the 1933 budget. Later budgets were prepared without the active direction or supervision of the governor. Except for a few instances in the first years of the Big Three, there is no evidence that the

[13] Other reorganizations were studied and suggested in other years, but the recommendations for action were not reflected in printed budgets (see below, Chapter 9).

governor attended budget hearings or conferences between the Commission of Administration and Finance and department heads.

On three occasions the governor-elect was not the incumbent. The influence of incoming Governor Floyd B. Olson is not discernible in the preparation of the 1931 budget. Six years later the budget reflects an apparent effort to "play up" some of Governor-elect Elmer A. Benson's tax proposals, but Benson's participation in the formulation of the budget estimates and recommended appropriations was negligible. When Harold E. Stassen was elected governor in the fall of 1938 he chose to ignore the budget commissioner's recommendations but took an active part in the preparation of his own brief recommendations to the legislature, aided by staff members of the Minnesota Institute of Governmental Research, a privately supported organization.

Only one governor, Stassen, emphasized the budget to the extent of delivering a budget message to the legislature in person.[14] In 1933 Governor Olson had written a comparatively brief letter on the budget problem to the legislature; this was printed in the budget document. There is no record of any other gubernatorial budget messages.

The governors could not, however, escape the necessity of mentioning certain budget problems in their inaugural messages. Each of these addresses contained some statements as to the governor's position on major appropriations and tax matters; the proportion of the message devoted to budget matters varied with the relative importance that the governor attached to this subject as compared to the other problems of state. Governor Christianson, whose watchword was economy, repeatedly referred to the work of the Big Three in reducing appropriation requests, evidently supporting them. The appropriations recommended by Governor Benson in the 1937 inaugural message were considerably out of line with the recommendations contained in the budget. The 1939 inaugural contained a statement that the governor did not agree with the budget proposed by the outgoing administration. With these two exceptions, there were no major differences between statements made in the inaugural messages and the printed budgets.

The part the governors have played in the legislative consideration of the budget can never be accurately known. Relation-

[14] February 1, 1939.

ships between the governor and the legislative leaders, informal conferences on pending legislation, and the several ways in which the governor influences action in both houses are not matters of record and are difficult to assess.

What can be ascertained, however, is the formal action of the governor in support of the budget after the legislature had acted. Although the governor had no power to raise appropriations or to make changes in the tax laws in the face of legislative opposition, he did have three courses of action by which he could back up recommendations for economy if the legislature exceeded the appropriations that he had recommended: (1) He could veto whole appropriation bills, necessitating further legislative action; (2) he could exercise an item veto over specific appropriations and approve the bills otherwise; and (3) through the allotment powers of the Big Three, he might have tried to prevent expenditure of the full appropriation. Because major appropriation and tax bills were usually passed at the end of the session, governors did not often veto entire bills, a practice that might have necessitated a special session. Governor Christianson made very effective use of his item veto power, however, to strike out appropriations that had not been recommended in the executive budget.[15] The third power, that of reducing allotments, was not commonly resorted to in a conscious attempt to preserve the original biennial budget recommendations; where the law increased an appropriation above the recommendations, the governors ordinarily took the attitude that the allotment powers should not be used to defeat an expressed legislative policy.

The Legislature and the Budget

Budgets were not formally presented to the legislature so as to be mentioned in the journals or to call for reference to a particular committee or committees. Nor did the governor or the Commission of Administration and Finance run the risk of incurring legislative displeasure (for "usurping" the "prerogatives" of legislators) by preparing budget bills for introduction into either house.

Appropriation matters are considered primarily by the Finance

[15] He used the item veto to strike out $1,836,160.84 in 1925 and $1,515,444.60 in 1927 and expressed regret that he did not have the constitutional authority to make a further cut by reducing individual items. In 1929 he used the same power to force the legislature to repass certain appropriations at a figure $556,000 lower than in the bill as orginally passed.

Committee in the Senate and by the Appropriations Committee in the House. Legislators who are not members of these two committees ordinarily have neither the time nor the inclination to delve deeply into budget matters, and therefore the action of these committees, and of joint conference committees in case of disputes, usually prevail. Both the House Appropriations Committee and the Senate Finance Committee have always held hearings with representatives of each department on their requested appropriations. The departments customarily defend their original requests before the legislative committees rather than uphold the budget recommendations. Departments also have felt free to present entirely new requests to the legislature if it suited them.[16] Except in 1931 and 1937 the total appropriations passed by the legislature always exceeded the recommendations in the budget.[17]

The House Appropriations Committee usually made use of the biennial budget prepared for them. The budget document ordinarily lay on their desks; it was consulted frequently with respect to the recommendations for the several appropriation items; the budget commissioner was ordinarily invited to appear before the committee near the beginning of the session in order to make an oral presentation of the budget; and members of the Big Three were sometimes called in later to clarify points arising with respect to the budget. In 1937 an examiner of the comptroller's division who had served on the temporary staff preparing the biennial budget was appointed clerk of the Appropriations Committee for the legislative session.

The Senate Finance Committee exhibited an entirely different attitude. From the very beginning the Senate committee refused to use the detailed budget document. It had found the summary booklet printed for the legislature just before the adoption of the reorganization act rather useful, and so the printing of this document was continued. This summary contained in very brief form

[16] The budget commissioner, in his 1938 budget handbook for departments, instructed departments and officials to submit all requests for appropriations to the budget commissioner for transmittal to the governor and the legislature. The governors apparently never attempted to get departments to support the executive budget figures before legislative committees, nor did they ever succeed in stopping departments from submitting new requests directly to the legislature without routing them through the budget commissioner.

[17] In 1937 the legislature exceeded the recommendations on a large number of specific appropriations, but cut below the budget on university, educational, and building appropriations, so the totals were less than Rasmussen's recommendations. Leg-

a list of the direct revenue fund appropriations made by the preceding legislature, the amounts of departmental requests for appropriations for the next biennium, blank spaces for writing in committee action, and, after 1925, the budget commissioner's recommendations for revenue fund appropriations.[18] The Senate committee also made frequent use of the biennial report of the state auditor, which contains tables showing receipts, appropriations, and disbursements for preceding years, with breakdowns by agencies

islative action on budget recommendations over a ten-year period is shown in the following table:

DEPARTMENTAL REQUESTS, BUDGET RECOMMENDATIONS, AND LEGISLATIVE APPROPRIATIONS FROM THE GENERAL REVENUE FUND FOR THE FISCAL YEARS 1928–39*

Fiscal Years	First Year	Second Year	Total for Biennium
1928 and 1929			
Departmental requests......$24,431,380.14		$23,146,170.03	$47,577,550.17
Recommendations of budget			
commissioner 19,348,028.00		19,582,735.00	38,930,763.00
Legislative appropriations ... 19,733,718.00		19,899,415.00	39,633,133.00
1930 and 1931			
Departmental requests....... 23,106,442.05		21,734,772.32	44,841,214.37
Recommendations of budget			
commissioner 20,521,674.00		20,005,611.00	40,527,285.00
Legislative appropriations ... 20,844,160.79		20,233,271.00	41,077,431.79
1932 and 1933			
Departmental requests 25,898,030.56		23,876,980.04	49,775,010.60
Recommendations of budget			
commissioner 22,722,869.32		21,177,817.00	43,900,686.32
Legislative appropriations ... 21,109,353.18		20,465,460.00	41,574,813.18
1934 and 1935			
Departmental requests....... 22,522,465.52		22,270,876.95	44,793,342.47
Recommendations of budget			
commissioner 18,027,761.85		18,316,226.95	36,343,988.80
Legislative appropriations ... 18,083,203.67		18,550,690.00	36,633,893.67
1936 and 1937			
Departmental requests....... 26,106,947.73		24,019,892.36	50,126,840.09
Recommendations of budget			
commissioner 19,607,989.23		21,337,191.86	40,945,181.09
Legislative appropriations ... 21,418,493.69		21,783,521.15	43,202,014.84
1938 and 1939			
Departmental requests....... †		†	62,164,060.57
Recommendations of budget			
commissioner 29,084,555.00		29,549,891.00	58,634,446.00
Legislative appropriations ... 29,300,764.10		28,810,061.00	58,110,825.10

* Table prepared by C. E. Axness, budget examiner in the Minnesota Department of Administration. Deficiency appropriations are not included (cf. Ch. 5, p. 83).

† Figures showing department requests for each year not available.

[18] This summary contained no details of the way the money was used, the purposes of the requests, or the bases of the recommendations. It contained no information on any of the state's funds except the general revenue fund. One of its chief virtues in the minds of senators was the provision for blank spaces which the legislators could use for writing in the allowances made by their committee.

and items of expenditure, including individual salaries. The budget itself, however, was of little importance to the Senate Finance Committee and members of the Commission of Administration and Finance appeared before the committee only on rare occasions.[19]

Each house had its own tax committee for the consideration of revenue-raising measures. Since the budget did not contain revenue recommendations in the early years, these committees had no occasion to refer to it. Although some of the later budgets contained tax recommendations, the Minnesota Tax Commission's report, rather than the budget, received the major attention of these committees. Only once or twice did members of the Big Three appear before the regular tax committees of the legislature.

Although the legislative rules called for all appropriation bills to be reported out to the floor within sixty legislative days from the opening of the session, even major appropriation bills were often introduced late in the session, and debate upon and final passage of the appropriations usually took place in the last week and often the last night of the session. Since the fiction was maintained that taxes were dependent on appropriations, the property-tax bill was also one of the last measures to be passed each session. The practice of delaying action on appropriations meant not only that the bills were often adopted in a hurry but also that the public was often uninformed as to the actual financial legislation that was approved. On one occasion the budget commissioner published a summary of such legislation at the end of the session.[20]

[19] Exceptions occurred in 1929, when members of the Big Three were invited to defend their action in reducing university appropriation requests, and in 1933, when the budget commissioner attended a number of the committee's public hearings and sometimes gave her views on the appropriation requests.

[20] In 1933. In 1939 a synopsis of current legislation to date was published (in mimeographed form) by the budget commissioner as of February 1, March 1, and April 1, but no final summary appeared after the end of the session.

Chapter 5

EXPENDITURE CONTROL

THE heart of the movement for the establishment of the Commission of Administration and Finance was the desire for a continuous economy and efficiency commission that would have the power, under the governor, to supervise and control the expenditures of all state departments, officials, and agencies. Though there was probably little expectation that the commissioners themselves would be "efficiency experts," it was generally expected that the commission with its staff would be a positive factor in eliminating unnecessary and undesirable expenditures.

The commission's efforts at expenditure control were characterized as follows: (1) The system never gave the commission a real control over the incurring of expenditures, primarily because accrual accounting procedures were lacking; (2) at times actions of the governor's office and other divisions of the Big Three operated to weaken the expenditure control process; (3) the commission's supervision over expenditures undoubtedly caused irritations among departments, but very few major clashes occurred; (4) even though it was not fully effective, supervision over allotments and pre-audits had a helpful, restraining influence on expenditures; and (5) apart from its powers of supervision and control, the commission was able to effect economies on its own initiative and through persuasive influences on the departments.

The System Outlined by Law

Several means of expenditure supervision and control were given to the Commission of Administration and Finance by the act of 1925. The commission of course had the opportunity to effect economies through its personnel powers, centralized purchasing, and supervision of printing. But in addition to these powers the commission had general authority over all expenditures of the state departments and institutions under its control.[1]

One section of the reorganization act stated that "the commis-

---

[1] The commission's statutory powers to effect economies may be classed as of two types: (1) to secure economies through reducing unit costs — as in purchasing, salary schedules, etc.; and (2) to secure economies through reducing or eliminating the acquisition of goods or services — as in allotment control.

sion shall have the power to supervise and control the . . . expenditures of the several officials, departments, and agencies of the state government and of the institutions under their control . . . and the creation or incurrence of all financial . . . obligations." [2]

A key to the type of control expected is shown in the following:

No appropriation to any official, department, or agency of the state government or to any institution under its control shall become available for expenditure thereby during any quarterly period of the fiscal year, or other less than quarterly period thereof fixed by rule of the commission, until such official, department, agency, or institution shall have submitted to the commission an estimate in advance, in such form as the commission may prescribe, for such quarterly or other period, as the case may be, next ensuing of the amount required for each activity to be carried on and each purpose for which money is to be expended during said period, and until such estimate shall have been approved by the commission. Accounts shall be kept and reports rendered showing the expenditure for each such purpose.

The commission may approve estimates covering salaries and other fixed expenditures for a longer period than three months. It also shall have authority to modify or amend any estimate previously approved by it under such rules as it may prescribe.[3]

To make sure that departments would not incur obligations in excess of the amounts so approved by the commission the law contained the following provisions:

The Comptroller shall keep such books of account as shall be necessary to properly carry out the provisions of this act. . . . [Section 10]

No official, department, or agency of the state government or institution under its control shall enter into any contract, agreement, or obligation involving the expenditure of money unless or until the Comptroller shall first certify that there is a balance in the appropriation from which such obligation is required to be paid which is not otherwise encumbered to meet obligations previously incurred. [Section 13]

The State Auditor shall examine every account, bill, claim, and demand against the state, and if previously authorized by the commission and if otherwise a legal and proper claim he shall approve the same and issue his warrant in payment thereof. . . . [Section 11]

Quarterly Allotments

Quarterly allotment requests [4] were initiated by the various departments on forms provided by the Department of Administra-

---

[2] Art. III, Sec. 3.

[3] Art. III, Sec. 5. It appeared from other sections of the act that "appropriation" here meant both direct appropriations by the legislature and reappropriated receipts. This meaning was never seriously questioned by any department.

[4] The term "quarterly allotments" is here used to describe the allotment system, even though, after 1929, allotments were made for two quarters at a time and in

tion and Finance. The request detailed the estimated expenditures for the next quarter from each appropriation account, according to a uniform classification of expenditures. Opposite each requested figure were blank spaces for the commission to note its action— approving, reducing, or disallowing the estimates. After a few years the commission asked the departments to include with each allotment budget salary schedules in support of their request for personal service expenditures, and other explanatory material in support of other requests. In the last two years, 1937–39, the commission also required a statement of estimated receipts to be a part of the allotment budgets for all accounts that received income from other sources than from a direct appropriation.

One clue to the minuteness of supervision attempted is the itemization that was required in the allotments. Originally a classification of about sixty items was set up; from time to time minor changes were made until it contained about seventy items; in 1937, a new classification of thirty-seven items was substituted.[5] No appropriation was ever split up into that many parts, however; in the first years the classification was not strictly followed and many big accounts were divided into from three to five items; even when in later years the classification was strictly observed, the average appropriation was divided into six or seven items.

The commission's decision on allotment requests was usually based upon two factors: the need for apportioning the available resources of the department over the whole fiscal year,[6] and the commission's opinion as to the desirability and need of releasing the amounts requested for the various expenditures.[7] That opinion

reality became semiannual allotments. The term "preview budget" was used commonly in communications from the budget commissioner to department heads with reference to quarterly allotments.

[5] In 1931, after a six months' review of expenditure abstracts of the Rural Credit Department, the budget commissioner issued special income and expenditure abstract forms for this department and classifications of objects of expenditure for the two funds from which the department drew its support. The commissioner reported that, with the resulting itemization of expenditures, operating costs dropped so suddenly and in such large amounts as to prove former abuses.

[6] This meant that at the beginning of each allotment period, except the last in each fiscal year, there was to be reserved a sufficient portion of each appropriation to sustain that activity for the remainder of the year. The same principle applied to accounts which had dedicated income. In ordinary cases this meant 25 per cent, 50 per cent, or 75 per cent of the year's resources; in the case of seasonal activities, however, discretion was used.

[7] The decision on allotments did not depend directly upon available receipts; when income was low, a tendency for economy might be more pronounced, but the allot

would be based upon the amounts used for a similar purpose in the corresponding period of the preceding year, explanations given by the departments for their requests, knowledge gained through observation of the expenditure voucher warrants of the department, information disclosed in the postaudits, and sometimes personal field visits of commission members or employees.[8] The exact factors that influenced the decisions varied of course at different times, depending upon whose allotment was under consideration and who was passing upon the allotments. The first commission attempted to act on allotments as a body, but after a time the budget commissioner took over this work for the commission.[9]

In the approval of each allotment request the Department of Administration and Finance reserved the right to change it by further amendment or modification. Two types of amendments were used during most of the commission's fourteen years. One was a transfer of allotments, whereby a department could secure a shift of unused balances between allotment items of an appropriation.[10] The other was a supplemental release, by means of which an allotment for any given period could be increased.[11] Transfers were allowed upon showing of cause; supplements were supposed to be reserved for unforeseen emergencies. Actually a large number of transfers and sup-

ment system was not used to effect a balance in revenue fund operations. (That is, a fall of nondedicated income 7 per cent below the total appropriations did not result in a 7 per cent hold-back in allotments of revenue fund appropriations.) Allotments, of course, were customarily kept within the amounts available to departments through direct appropriations or through reappropriated receipts; no disbursements could lawfully be made in excess of such appropriations or receipts.

[8] The commission never attempted to reduce expenditures for fixed charges, grants-in-aid, or other items of that nature. The power to reduce allotments was exercised solely with respect to appropriations (including reappropriated receipts), the spending of which was discretionary with executive or administrative officials.

[9] Sometimes budget commissioners gained attention in the press with news of clipping a half-million or a million dollars from allotment requests. On the other hand, it might have been possible for a budget commissioner to have cut the requests very little, if he had gained the confidence of the departments prior to submission of the allotments, and persuaded the departments to submit low, uninflated requests. It is not possible to say accurately how much was saved through the allotment system, because a reduced budget might have been increased later with supplements (which were never announced to the newspapers), and too, there is no reason to believe that every department would actually have spent every dollar in its original request, if it had been allowed.

[10] This was not a power to transfer moneys from one appropriation to another — a power which no administrative or executive official possessed (with the exception of a few appropriations).

[11] The supplement did not add to the total appropriation — it merely added to one allotment and had the effect of reducing the balance available for future allotments (within the appropriation limits).

plements were released in nearly every allotment period.[12] A third type of amendment, which had the effect of reducing an allotment after the money had once been released, was very seldom used; only in 1939 was a form provided for this purpose, and then it was used primarily at the request of departments in order to secure a shift of funds from one allotment period to another.

A substantial number of the supplemental releases and allotment transfers were made solely on the initiative of the various departments, but in later years quite a few were prompted by some division of the Big Three. The personnel division especially was concerned with placing people at work, whether or not money had been provided in the quarterly budgets. The purchasing division, too, often persuaded departments to buy more, regardless of the budget.[13]

Although the allotment system represented the commission's most powerful means of control over departments, minor irritations rather than important clashes arose out of its operation. The university lawsuit [14] was the only one of the commission's Supreme Court cases involving a contest over the allotment power,[15] and it revolved around a more serious consideration of the whole relation of an administrative control agency to the Board of Regents. Some of the commission's minor conflicts were related to an exercise of the allotment power, but in general either the commission failed to hamper operating departments seriously by its use of the allotment power, or the operating departments were able to secure a modification or circumvention of any important restrictions that the commission might have imposed.[16]

[12] Budget commissioners repeatedly complained to department heads about the excessive number of requests for supplemental releases and transfers. Commissioner Rasmussen, in a letter dated October 12, 1936, stated that so many requests of this nature had been received that, if allowed, they would virtually nullify the budget allotments for the first six months of that year.

[13] Especially during the periods when economy was not one of the primary objectives of the governor, the following were possible reasons for this attitude on the part of the purchasing commissioner: (1) The purchasing commissioner had no particular incentive for economy; (2) even if he were sincerely anxious to obtain economical unit prices, he had no particular incentive to reduce the quantity of state purchases; (3) it may have been politically desirable to secure more business for certain friendly firms, which would necessitate persuading departments to requisition more of the supplies; and (4) the purchasing commissioner was subject to the influence of salesmen calling on him every week in an effort to get the state to give them new or additional business.

[14] See above, Chapter 2, pages 25–27.

[15] The Railroad and Warehouse Commission case (see Chapter 2, page 21) arose out of the system, but was a contest over the salary-fixing power.

[16] This is not a criticism of the commission, nor is it necessarily an indication that the allotment system was not an important instrument for economy. The mere pres-

EXPENDITURE CONTROL

There were exceptions to the whole allotment procedure. Expenditures for the legislature and the district court judges, grants to various agricultural societies, debt service, and trust-fund transactions were never formally allotted in advance.[17] The university expenditures were not subject to the allotment process after 1928, and later on, opinions of the attorney general exempted relief expenditures and Rural Credit Department payments from allotment control. Institutions under the Board of Control submitted quarterly allotment budgets, but through the commission's choice they were not observed or enforced until 1937.[18]

Budgetary Accounting

A system of budgetary accounting was necessary in order to enforce and check up on the operation of the allotment system. Only by keeping such accounts would there be a means of holding expenditures within allotted amounts. Some system was also necessary because in accordance with the law the state auditor would approve and pay voucher warrants only when the commission certified that the claims to be paid by the warrants had been properly authorized.

It was therefore arranged to enter the various budget allotments, as they were approved, on an allotment-and-disbursement ledger and to record group totals of voucher warrants against the proper allotments when they were received for payment.[19] To make certain

ence of the allotment system, the requirement that departments plan, at least to some extent, their operations and future expenditures, and the necessity for departments to explain their proposed expenditures to some authority — all these undoubtedly served as an important restraining influence in favor of economy and efficiency.

An exception to the general rule on this point may be noted during the difficult years of 1932–33, when Commissioner Wittich reduced allotments by $750,000 in one six-month period (July 1 to December 31, 1932). Mrs. Wittich, in a statement released to the press at the time she announced her intention to resign in March 1933, described her office as a "storm center" during a period when declining revenues forced vigorous use of her expenditure control power.

[17] These expenditures were made by warrants drawn directly by the state auditor without vouchers being submitted by any other state official. The nature of these expenditures did not admit of administrative control.

[18] In 1935 the legislature specifically authorized the Board of Control to exceed its appropriation for the first year of the 1935–37 biennial period in anticipation of a supplemental appropriation (*Session Laws*, 1935, Ch. 159, Sec. 22; opinion of the attorney general, March 26, 1936).

[19] It will be recalled that the reorganization act, on the other hand, had apparently contemplated recording obligations *when they were incurred* and keeping a record of unencumbered balances. The only situation where encumbrances were recorded was in the case of construction contracts written by the commission itself, on which a memorandum record of the obligations was kept.

that the appropriation accounts would not be overdrawn, it was also found necessary to keep an appropriation ledger. Both ledgers were kept with bookkeeping machines in the offices of the Department of Administration and Finance.

Since departments needed allotment accounting records also, a series of forms were drawn up to be used by the departments in posting budgetary accounts by hand. These forms followed the same principle that was used in the central control accounts—posting voucher warrants against the approved allotments when disbursements were made.

The weakness of this system is evident: The point of "control" was established too far along in the expenditure process to allow much control—the check against excessive spending was made when bills were ready for payment rather than when obligations were to be incurred. When the proposed payments exceeded approved allotments the commission found it almost necessary to approve a supplemental allotment, since the bills had already been incurred. And if the commission did not approve a supplemental allotment and pass the payment, the department merely waited until the next allotment period and then placed the bills in line for payment against the new allotment.[20] Even more serious than the opportunity to exceed allotments was the fact that this type of accounting procedure allowed the departments to incur obligations in excess of appropriations set by law.[21]

Time after time the Commission of Administration and Finance called the attention of the departments to the provisions of the law and the necessity of watching obligations at the point where they were incurred. Twice the commission provided that on each requisition for purchase the departments should certify that unencumbered funds were available to pay the bill. At one time the budget commissioner placed on the operating department's copy of supplemental allotments, as they were approved, a request to check books

[20] For a time, especially under the first commission when new allotments were made every three months, this procedure went undetected by the Big Three. If necessary, vendors cooperated by postdating invoices.

[21] An extreme example is the State Tourist Bureau, which is operated entirely on direct appropriations. It had an appropriation of $40,000 for the fiscal year ending June 30, 1937; at the end of that year it had $28.11 left in the appropriation and known bills amounting to $27,379.73. Thus more than half of the next year's appropriation was used to pay old bills. Deficiency appropriations resulted frequently from this same procedure; departments could incur expenses in excess of appropriations, carry bills over from one fiscal year to another, and when the accumulation of unpaid bills grew large, it would ask the legislature for a deficiency appropriation.

EXPENDITURE CONTROL

closely enough to ask for supplements or allotment transfers, if necessary, in advance of purchases. In 1937 the legislature added a new rider to the state department appropriations bill clearly making the appropriations subject to the reorganization act and providing that no obligation should be entered into in excess of unencumbered balances.[22] But as long as the bookkeeping was done on a completely cash basis, departments found it easy to incur expenses in excess of approved allotments and appropriations.

The commission took a step toward correcting this situation in the fiscal year 1937–38, when it provided that the budgetary accounts should be changed from a "strictly-cash" basis to a "cash-and-accrual" basis. All departments were instructed to keep records of obligations when they were incurred, and in both the departmental and the administration and finance budgetary control accounts all payments after June 30, 1938, were charged to the allotment quarter in which the bills were incurred, regardless of when they were paid. This change still did not provide for central accounting control of obligations when they were incurred,[23] but it did bring about a considerable reduction in the violations of the law with respect to incurring obligations in excess of funds. An equally important fact was that this change made it possible for the first time to compile information concerning state expenditures on an accrual basis.[24]

[22] *Session Laws*, 1937, Ch. 457, Sec. 39.

[23] After 1933 the Commission of Administration and Finance at no time had an appropriation large enough to enable it to incur the extra expense of installing an accrual accounting system (see Chapter 3, pages 60–61). In the 1937 and 1939 budgets, however, it requested a special appropriation for that purpose.

[24] The deficiency appropriation record during the commission's existence is as follows.

Fiscal Years	Department Request	Budget Recommendation	Legislative Appropriation
1928 and 1929	$710,034.90	$701,334.90	$997,201.28
1930 and 1931	677,361.47	677,361.47	1,170,464.04
1932 and 1933	574,300.00	574,300.00	1,633,507.40
1934 and 1935	....	....	573,107.18
1936 and 1937	324,000.00	324,000.00	730,982.90
1938 and 1939	2,832,953.51	3,285,719.97	1,653,482.10

It should be noted that the legislature specifically authorized the Board of Control to incur a deficiency in 1936 and 1937 (*Session Laws*, 1935, Ch. 159, Sec. 22). A $2,000,000 deficiency appropriation for relief was voted in 1937 (*ibid.*, 1937, Ch. 209), which is not shown in the above table. Furthermore, appropriations for legislative salaries and expenses, printing of the *Session Laws* and the *Legislative Manual*, new activities for which funds were made immediately available, and payment of claims are included in the deficiency appropriations.

COMMISSION OF ADMINISTRATION AND FINANCE

Control through Pre-audit

Another device for expenditure control was the commission's authority to scan and review disbursement documents before payments were made on them—a power commonly called the pre-audit.[25] Disbursements were subject to the following procedure: The operating department prepared combination voucher warrants for each payee and sent them, together with supporting documents and an abstract (a listing and classification) of the expenditures to the Department of Administration and Finance; the Big Three kept one copy of the abstract and sent the remainder to the state auditor; the state auditor, after auditing the claims, signed the voucher warrants and sent them with a copy of the abstract to the state treasurer, filing the rest of the documents; and the state treasurer countersigned the warrants and they became negotiable instruments, which were then sent to the respective payees.

The purpose of the commission's pre-audit[26] was originally threefold: to see that the purchases, salaries, and other items had been authorized by the Big Three; to verify the classification of the expenditures in accordance with the budgetary accounting system; and to make sure that the disbursements were within the approved quarterly allotments and supplementary releases. In practice the pre-audit also served as (1) a means of checking prices and taking cash discounts on some purchases; (2) a device to enforce certain rules, such as the travel-expense regulations; and (3) a way of securing detailed information on departmental spending that could be of value in passing judgment upon future budgets.

The commission could not use the pre-audit of disbursements to substitute its judgment for that of a department on whether

[25] The word *pre-audit* has three possible uses with reference to expenditures:

(1) Referring to the preview of expenditures afforded in the submission of quarterly allotments. The allotment system was often incorrectly referred to as the "pre-audit" in Minnesota state government circles in 1925 and the years immediately following. A brief study of an allotment budget is hardly an audit. The term pre-audit is no longer used in this sense.

(2) Referring to a check of original expenditure documents (requisitions, orders on the store, requests for travel authorization, etc.) before obligations are incurred. An administrative pre-audit must be made in this manner if it is to be more effective for *control* purposes. The term pre-audit has not been used in this sense in Minnesota state government, however.

(3) Referring to a review of disbursement documents, after expense has been incurred, but before payment is made. This is an audit of documents preparatory to making payment. The term is most often used in this sense and is so used here.

[26] In this chapter the pre-audit is discussed in its relation to expenditure control; in Chapter 6 it is discussed in its relation to the whole auditing function.

or not a given expenditure should be made. By the time the voucher warrant reached the commission offices the obligation had been incurred, the goods or services had been received, and the commission could not halt the expenditure unless it was in excess of funds or improper for some other sufficient reason. A review of the proposed expenditures in advance, in the form of a pre-audit of purchase requisitions and other documents resulting in the creation of encumbrances, would have offered a better opportunity to stop certain expenditures in the interests of economy, but this method was never tried.

Nevertheless, the administrative pre-audit of disbursements helped effect various economies. Numerous cash discounts on purchases, which had been overlooked by the departments, were secured. Excessive expenses on travel reimbursement vouchers were cut down to conform to the rules. Vouchers in excess of the state printer's approved invoices were reduced to the proper amounts. Most important of all—in the last three years at least—was the fact that on the basis of facts disclosed in the pre-audit the budget and accounting division was able to negotiate with departments, looking toward economies in the future on certain items.[27]

The greatest weakness of the pre-audit was its incompleteness. In practice the state auditor determined the form of the voucher warrant and the other documents that had to be filed with it, and the pre-audit of the institutions under the Board of Control was ineffective because the auditor never required supporting information on their expenditures. Vouchers for payments on highway contracts were never accompanied by any supporting documents. Until 1937–38, when the Department of Administration and Finance asked for them, the Highway Department did not submit purchase orders with its voucher warrants. After 1928 the university disbursements were not subject to pre-audit, and subsequently relief expenditures were removed for a time from scrutiny of the Big Three.

Economies on Particular Expenditures

Commission members at times found successful methods of securing economy and efficiency apart from the allotment control

[27] There is some evidence, not subject to complete verification, that on occasions the pre-audit power was used as a club to force departments to make purchases and to procure fidelity and surety bonds of firms favored by one or more members of the Big Three.

powers. Studies of particular objects of expenditure often prompted economies. Both the budget commissioners and the comptrollers were anxious to reduce costs where practicable.

Travel regulations, for example, were promulgated by the first commission to bring down the cost of travel by state employees. A study of telephone costs at the capitol revealed high toll charges for necessary calls to Minneapolis; installation of Minneapolis trunk lines on the capitol switchboard saved money. The first comptroller cut thousands of dollars from the cost of the *Legislative Manual* ("Blue Book") by rearrangement of its contents.

In 1932, when the costs at the capitol's power and light plant became an object of attention, the budget commissioner, Mrs. Wittich, wrote the departments in the capitol group requesting the cooperation of employees in turning off unneeded lights and in avoiding waste of heat; [28] she reported it brought a saving of from three to six tons of coal a day in the operation of the plant. A study of fidelity and surety bonds brought savings by writing blanket policies for a group of positions on a two-year basis. Checking and certification of pay rolls permitted the control of unnecessary employments and unauthorized salary increases.[29]

During the years 1936, 1937, and 1938 further economies were made. A study of state advertising revealed some unnecessary publications of legal notices, which were thereafter omitted. Purchase of state-owned cars was placed under scrutiny, and reports on the use of such cars were instituted, resulting in savings to the various departments. A study of rented real property was followed by installation of a rent memorandum system, which brought about lower prices on some of the rented quarters and abandonment of others. New travel regulations helped cut "subsistence expenses" of traveling state employees still further.

Studies of particular departments also revealed opportunities for small economies. The first commissioners specialized to some extent in studying departments with a view to possible savings. In 1932 the budget commissioner and comptroller made separate studies of the Rural Credit Department that resulted in changes in operation and a legislative reorganization of the department in 1933. In 1936 the budget commissioner sent an employee on a two-week visit to the Minnesota state teachers' colleges for the

[28] Letter of December 9, 1932.
[29] Cf. Chapter 8, page 122.

purpose of studying problems of organization and financial management; numerous suggestions for minor changes and economies were adopted by several colleges as a result of the visit.

The Governor and Expenditure Control

Although the Commission of Administration and Finance was by law a staff agency of the governor for dealing with state departments, the governor as chief executive was also responsible for seeing that the laws were faithfully executed by the operating departments. Lest the finance department exercise so much power over the other departments as to restrict them from properly carrying out their duties the reorganization act had provided that the departments could appeal to the governor from decisions of the Big Three, and he could overrule his appointees.[30]

There is no record indicating that this provision of the law was ever formally called into play. So long as the Commission of Administration and Finance, or more particularly the budget commissioner, was willing to give consideration to department heads, it was not necessary. And if there was an unsettled difference of opinion on an important subject, an informal contact with the governor's office and a suggestion to the Big Three probably took care of the situation. Nor is there any record that the governor used the commission's expenditure control powers, as he might have, to obstruct the work of a department head with whom he was politically at odds.

During the first half of its existence the commission found support for its expenditure control program in the governor's office. One of Governor Christianson's administrative policies was economy, and he was not ready to intervene often against the decision of his "finance board."[31] Referring to the allotment system in an address at Hutchinson on October 2, 1928, formally opening his campaign for reelection, the governor said: "If a proposed expenditure is for a customary or usual project, it is allowed as a matter of routine. If it is unusual, if it embarks the state in a new enterprise or commits it to a new activity, it is scrutinized. If the finance board rejects it, the department head has the right of appeal to the

---

[30] *Session Laws*, 1925, Ch. 426, Art. III, Sec. 15.

[31] The governor, however, vigorously refuted the charge that his economy program had injured state agencies and institutions. In his farewell message to the legislature (January 7, 1931) he pointed with pride to the increased facilities and effective management of the state institutions under the Board of Control.

governor. Surely, if the chief executive of this state is to have anything to say about the administration for which he is responsible,
he ought to have the power to determine whether the men he
appoints should be permitted to commit the state to enlarged programs that will call for an increased budget." [32]

Governor Olson himself took the lead in the matter of expenditure control in 1932, when he addressed a request to all state
departments and agencies to give their employees payless vacations
in June of that year as a means of saving the state approximately
$570,000.[33] The university, which would have accounted for almost
40 per cent of the total savings, refused to do so at the time, though
they did effect a somewhat similar salary reduction the following
fiscal year. The Executive Council, Supreme Court, secretary of
state, state auditor, state treasurer, banking division, State Employees' Retirement Association, and four examining boards refused
to cooperate in the governor's plan;[34] all other departments and
their employees joined in to save $325,000. No attempt was made
to force the payless vacation on the noncooperating departments.

In the latter half of the commission's history the governor's office
did not directly oppose the commission on matters concerning the
control of expenditures, but often made decisions that upset and
undermined the system. This was especially true when the governor's office authorized or directed a department to do something
involving a new outlay of money, regardless of the Big Three's
established budget allotments. Salaries were especially troublesome,
because the governor's office frequently decided that jobs should
be made for certain applicants or even large groups of applicants,
even though the allotment did not provide for them. Purchases were
sometimes made from certain vendors in excess of budgets; a notable case was a very large order for fire extinguishers, not even on
requisition when the purchase order was made in 1937–38. Even in

[32] Campaign document in the files of Minnesota Historical Society.
[33] Form letters of May 21, 1932, and June 7, 1932, signed by the governor. The original plan of having all permanent employees join in giving up half a month's salary would have resulted in a saving of more than $668,000. This was modified in the second letter so that employees receiving less than $1,200 should voluntarily give up only one week's salary, and other employees voluntarily give up two weeks' salary. It was pointed out that no state law granted any vacations to state employees, and that in view of the staggering of employment in private industry at the time no com-plaint should result.
[34] Information from a report of Budget Commissioner Wittich to Governor Olson. Note that all department heads refusing to cooperate were politically independent of the governor except the banking commissioner.

1939 a map-survey agreement with the federal government, involving expenditures by several state agencies, was made with the approval of the governor but without reference to the budgets.

In the earlier years the governor's leadership and direction on matters of expenditures were exercised through the commission, whereas in later years the governor's wishes on expenditures were often made known to the operating departments before the commission learned of them.

Chapter 6

AUDITING AND SUPERVISION OF ACCOUNTING

THE reorganization act did not disturb the duties of the state auditor with respect to accounting and auditing but added certain other accounting and auditing responsibilities to the duties of the Commission of Administration and Finance. The actual operations in this field deserve particular attention because some of the changes suggested in the administrative structure after 1935 emphasized possible alterations in the distribution of these duties.

A study of the auditing and accounting supervision as set up in the law and carried out in practice reveals the following: (1) The law made careful distinctions in the distribution of auditing and accounting duties, so that there would be neither duplication nor conflict in the work; (2) the auditing of state disbursements, achieved principally through pre-audit, was not completely effective; (3) the auditing of state receipts, achieved primarily through postaudit, was reasonably effective, with a few possible exceptions; (4) the auditing of the financial transactions and accounts of local units of government was reasonably satisfactory, though it bore little relationship to the principal purposes of the Big Three; and (5) improvements were frequently made in the accounting records and systems of the operating departments, but the important central accounting records of the auditor were not modernized correspondingly.

Distinction in Auditing and Accounting Duties

Several types of auditing and accounting duties may be distinguished from one another—the administrative pre-audit of disbursements, the legal pre-audit of disbursements, the current audit of receipts, the postaudit of financial transactions and accounts, proprietary and appropriation accounting, budgetary and allotment accounting, and the supervision of departmental accounting.

The administrative pre-audit of state disbursements was a function of the Commission of Administration and Finance. This pre-audit comprised a review of disbursement documents, preceding their execution, from the point of view of whether the transactions had been properly authorized, were advisable, and were within the expenditure limitations and rules that had been set by administrative authority.

The legal pre-audit of disbursements was retained as a duty of the state auditor by the reorganization act, which provided that he should "examine every account, bill, claim, and demand against the state, and if previously authorized by the Commission and if otherwise a legal and proper claim, he shall approve the same and issue his warrant in payment thereof in the manner provided by law."[1] The same section of the law gave the comptroller, chairman of the Big Three, a right to review the actions of the auditor in approving or disapproving claims, either on his own initiative or on an appeal by an interested party.

A "current audit" of receipts corresponds to a pre-audit of disbursements. Where a current audit of receipts is in effect, the central accounting officer examines receipt documents (duplicate receipts, departmental billings for services, records of licenses and permits issued, etc.) before "covering" the incoming moneys into the treasury. The responsibility for making a current audit of receipts was not expressly provided by law, though it could have been implied from the authority of the state auditor to control all payments into the treasury.

The postaudit of financial transactions and accounts of state and local governments, which had rested with the public examiner for some decades, was transferred to the comptroller when the public examiner's office was abolished by the reorganization act.[2] The postaudit may include not only a review of completed transactions but also an examination of the accounts, an inspection of records, and a check of cash, investments, and public property in the custody of the various officers and employees. The entire commission shared with the comptroller the authority "at any time to examine the accuracy and legality of all accounts, receipts, and expenditures of state monies and the use or disposition of state property."[3]

The reorganization act made no change at all in the state auditor's traditional duties of keeping the central accounts of the state with respect to receipts, disbursements, and appropriations. The laws of the state have long provided that the treasurer should be

---

[1] *Session Laws*, 1925, Ch. 426, Art. III, Sec. 11.

[2] Before 1925 there had also been a special Board of Audit, composed of three elective officials serving ex officio, which was responsible for a postaudit of the state treasurer. Its duties also were transferred to the comptroller.

[3] *Ibid.*, Sec. 3.

the custodian of moneys in the State Treasury and that the auditor should keep books of accounts reflecting the receipts and disbursements by funds, the status of appropriations made by law, and "such other accounts as shall be necessary to exhibit the condition of state finances from day to day." [4]

On the other hand, allotment and encumbrance accounts were to be kept centrally in the Department of Administration and Finance. The accounts to be kept by the auditor were for the purpose of reflecting the condition of the treasury and enforcing the legal accountability of the various officials; the budgetary accounts to be kept by the commission were for the purpose of providing a device to assist in the exercise of expenditure control. [5] The only item necessarily entering into both sets of central accounts was the disbursements, and since the auditor recorded them in totals by funds and appropriations, whereas the commission recorded them in more detail according to character and object, there was no real duplication of work or records. [6]

Supervision of the accounting done in the various state departments, formerly a duty of the public examiner, was transferred to the comptroller and the commission in 1925. In addition to the general language of the law transferring all the public examiner's duties to the comptroller, the reorganization act also specifically stated that "the Commission shall have the power to supervise and control the accounts . . . of the several officials, departments, and agencies of the state government and of the institutions under their control." [7]

Pre-auditing and Current Auditing

The responsibility of the state auditor for pre-auditing the disbursement of moneys from the state treasury was traditional in Minnesota and well established by statute. [8] The purpose of this

[4] *Mason's Minnesota Statutes,* 1927, Sec. 75.

[5] For a discussion of budgetary accounting practices, see above, Chapter 5, pages 81–83.

[6] The commission chose to keep an appropriation ledger of its own both so that it might have information readily at hand as to appropriation balances and so that there would be a control on the entries of disbursements to the allotment-and-disbursement ledger. The auditor also kept an appropriation ledger, and to some extent these duplicated each other.

[7] *Session Laws,* 1925, Ch. 426, Art. III, Sec. 3.

[8] *Mason's Minnesota Statutes,* 1927, Secs. 65–80. The constitution had simply provided that there should be an elective state auditor and that his duties should be prescribed by law. The argument has sometimes been advanced, however, that the pre-audit powers might be inferred from the constitution and that the pre-auditing

pre-audit was to interpose an advance check to ensure that all payments made from the treasury would be legal, proper, and in accordance with appropriations made by law. Along with this authority to examine and adjust demands on the treasury, the auditor also enjoyed the power to require the accounts against the state to be itemized, the authority to call for substantiating documents before making the disbursements, and the right to subpoena persons rendering accounts to the state.

Although as an independent elective official the auditor was thus responsible for making sure that the expenditures of administrative authorities conformed to the law, his pre-audit was not always thorough. For example, he accepted voucher warrants for the expenditures of state institutions on the basis of the Board of Control's approval without further audit.[9] Copies of purchase orders were not required on purchases made by departments other than the Big Three. Until late in 1938 payments on contracts were approved without checking the original contract or the balance due upon it.[10]

In its pre-audit the Commission of Administration and Finance reviewed the proposed disbursements from an administrative viewpoint and checked them against budget allotments for the various purposes.[11] The commission's certificate of release on all abstracts of expenditure that it forwarded to the state auditor stated that the expenditures represented therein had been authorized by the commission but that the certificate was not to be construed as an approval of the claims. This left the way open for the comptroller

duties could not be taken away, even if postauditing duties were substituted, by the legislature.

[9] This practice had originated when the Board of Control was created. The statute creating the board had provided that it should audit the expenditures of institutions once a month, forwarding an approved expense list to the auditor, and that the auditor should draw one warrant for the total expenses of each institution. When the voucher warrant system, requiring a separate voucher warrant for each payee, was substituted in 1917, and even when the 1925 reorganization act again directed the auditor to examine every claim against the state, he still followed the old practice of approving institution voucher warrants without copies of invoices or other substantiating evidence.

[10] The report of the architects' committee investigating the Bemidji Teachers' College project (see Chapter 2, page 44) said, "Not only has this department [state auditor] approved the payment of bills and the issuance of checks without having a record of contracts or contract amounts, but it has approved payments in excess of amounts due under contracts." Various irregularities and overpayments on highway contracts, discovered in 1939 investigations, also made it apparent that the legal pre-audit was not thorough enough to avoid all illegal payments.

[11] Cf. Chapter 5, pages 77–81.

93

to make a further legal pre-audit following the action of the auditor;[12] there is no record, however, that the comptroller ever used this power to review the action of the auditor before payment of bills.

Although both the auditor and the Department of Administration and Finance reviewed disbursement documents before the warrants were drawn upon the treasury, the audit was made from different viewpoints and did not necessarily represent a duplication of work or employees. No important conflicts resulted from this division of the pre-audit work; at times each office struck out or reduced the amounts of particular voucher warrants without interference from the other.

There never was a current audit of receipts. Payments into the state treasury could be made only upon drafts issued by the state auditor; in practice the auditor issued his draft upon the basis of letters or other reports from the departments informing him that a draft should be issued. The check as to whether or not all revenue-producing documents, such as licenses and permits, had been properly accounted for by the departments was left to the postaudit.

The Comptroller and the Postaudit

The comptroller exercised the duties of postauditing that had formerly belonged to the public examiner and the Board of Audit. The public examiner's responsibilities had included both the duty to "thoroughly examine" once a year the financial transactions and accounts of all state departments, officials, and agencies, and of societies receiving state aid, and the duty to conduct certain other examinations.[13] Counties and first-class cities were to be examined annually, and other cities, school districts, towns, and villages were to be audited upon request. Railroads and other companies paying

[12] Art. III, Sec. 11 of the reorganization act had provided that the auditor should pay claims only if they had been previously authorized by the commission, and it further provided that, after pre-audit by the state auditor, the comptroller might review the action of the auditor, either upon his own initiative or upon appeal by an interested party. An attorney general's opinion, rendered March 18, 1931, cast doubt upon the constitutionality of this provision for review of the auditor's decisions.

[13] *Mason's Minnesota Statutes*, 1927, Secs. 3274–86. Until November 1932 immediate responsibility for directing the staff of examiners engaged in postauditing was reposed in a deputy public examiner in the office of the comptroller, since the latter was engaged largely in the performance of the duties of chairman of the Big Three. Comptroller Pearlove, however, both because of his own experience and interest in auditing accounts and because of personal and political difficulties with the deputy examiner, A. R. Johnson (a hold-over from the Christianson administration and a friend of Governor Olson), abolished the position of deputy examiner with the governor's approval and assumed direct charge of postauditing work himself.

gross-earnings taxes to the state were to be examined regularly, and the public examiner had been charged with the duty of certifying to the Tax Commission the amount of their taxable earnings as disclosed by his audit. The sole duty of the Board of Audit had been the responsibility to audit and examine the accounts and books of the state treasurer at least four times a year without previous notice.

Audits of most state departments and agencies were made once every two years and some were made annually. A few were audited less often, while accounts of the state treasurer were usually audited regularly on the first of January and the first of July. Since expenditures had already been pre-audited by the state auditor and since the department employees did not actually handle cash in connection with the disbursement of funds, very little attention was paid to disbursements except to compile a classified list from the department records and verify the totals by reference to the auditor's ledgers. The examiners usually directed considerable attention toward the handling of cash receipts by the employees of the department that was subject to audit, and they also considered the adequacy of the methods used to account for state funds. During the years a number of shortages and irregularities were disclosed; recovery was usually secured, either through voluntary restitution or by legal action. All audit reports were made a matter of public record by the law.

The central accounting records of the state, kept by the state auditor, were subject to a less frequent and less comprehensive postaudit than the financial records of the departments. During most of this period an examination was made of the auditor's office only once in each biennium, and then the examination was customarily limited to merely verifying the accuracy of the general accounting records. The postaudit of the auditor's office was not regarded as an occasion for examining individual voucher warrants, not even all those that originated with the auditor such as vouchers for the payment of interest on the state debt. Neither was it regarded as an occasion for examining individual items of receipts, nor for verifying receivables, nor for studies of other financial transactions.

One of the problems that arose out of the organizational structure was that the comptroller was both the chairman of the Commission of Administration and Finance and the chief postauditing official, responsible for the examination of all the state's financial transactions, including those of the Big Three. The problem was simplified somewhat by the facts that the commission handled very little cash and that all state expenditures, including payments on purchase orders and contracts written by the commission, were subject to pre-audit by the independent, elective state auditor. In practice, the public examining division made a regular audit of the store division and special investigations of purchasing and printing on particular occasions. An examination of the entire Department of Administration and Finance covering the fiscal years 1926–29 was made by a member of the examining staff in the comptroller's office on August 15, 1929. Except for this instance, there was no postaudit of the Department of Administration and Finance.

The public examining division made fairly regular and complete audits of local subdivisions. According to the law the eighty-seven counties and the three first-class cities were to be examined once each calendar year. Actually the division was unable to make annual audits. Consequently the accounts of two or more years sometimes were covered in a single examination. Audits of other subdivisions were made when requested. These examinations usually included at least a sampling of financial transactions, as well as an audit of the accounting records, a verification of listed assets and liabilities, and an inquiry into the protection of public funds. The audits of local units of government disclosed a number of irregularities and were instrumental in securing the conviction of some local officials found guilty of embezzlement of funds and malfeasance in office.[14] The local audits sometimes injected the comptroller into controversies, however.[15]

[14] "A review of recent reports submitted by the Comptroller discloses that a large number of state, county, and other municipal officials have been removed from office for misappropriation of public funds, presenting of false claims, padding payrolls, etc. This has resulted not only in returning to the counties and other municipalities thousands of dollars, the theft of which might otherwise never have been detected, but the confidence of the people has been restored in the knowledge that public funds are being safeguarded. Further than this, with a staff of examiners experienced in municipal affairs, the Comptroller has been able to offer valuable advice to public officials, and make a study and analysis of the financial condition of the various municipalities which in many instances has resulted in placing the unit of government on a sound business-like basis" (*Report of Commission of Administration and Finance to the Legislature* [mimeographed], 1935).

[15] Several kinds of controversies occurred. Some local audits were initiated by a petition of a certain number of freeholders (in accordance with the statute) who were unfriendly to local officials then in office, and in such cases the audit report became a subject of local controversy. In other cases, where audits were made upon request

AUDITING AND ACCOUNTING

Records of the fifty to sixty largest taxpayers on a gross-earnings basis were examined annually, and as a result of the examinations additional taxes were collected on a number of occasions.

The postaudit of state departments and agencies was of practical value in connection with budget operations. Information appearing in regular audit reports, the presence of a trained staff from whom the budget division could borrow examiners familiar with state department finances, and the unquestioned investigatory authority of the public examining division [16]—all these were valuable in the preparation of the biennial budget. The postaudit of local units of government and of private corporations was not closely related to the other duties of the Department of Administration and Finance.[17]

The Independent Postaudit of 1927–28

A firm of certified public accountants, under direction of the attorney general, made an examination of the offices of the state auditor and the state treasurer in 1927–28, pursuant to an act of the 1927 legislature.[18] The act had been prompted by the disclosures that three employees of the two offices had been taking funds through manipulations dating as far back as 1920. Although the audit was by an independent firm of accountants,[19] the public examining division gave some assistance to the auditing staff, as was required.

The audit was limited in scope because the appropriation ($25,000) was not adequate enough to allow for a more comprehensive audit contract with the accounting firm. Attention was directed primarily toward accounting for cash transactions, checking the adequacy of the accounting system, and trying to verify the outstanding items on the auditor's general ledger. No attempt was

of the governing boards of the localities or where the audit was made annually according to law, the comptroller's findings criticizing the work of certain local officials would create friction. Another cause of controversy was the fact that local subdivisions were required to reimburse the comptroller's office for the cost of examinations, but they had no control over the cost; as a result they sometimes felt that the charges exceeded the value of the examination.

[16] The rights and privileges of the public examiner had become so well established that examiners could more readily secure information, especially from the offices of elective officials and the university, than could employees of other divisions of the relatively new Commission of Administration and Finance.

[17] There were obviously some advantages in placing all postauditing of public agencies in one department rather than setting up two organizations and two staffs, one for state agencies and one for the postaudit of local units of government.

[18] *Session Laws*, 1927, Ch. 430.

[19] See Chapter 2, page 24.

97

made to examine individual receipts or disbursements, to check their classification, nor to construct a balance sheet or operating statement for the state.

Considerable difficulty was encountered. Numerous discrepancies and errors in the auditor's reports were discovered. Lost drafts made it impossible to secure a correct list of outstanding drafts receivable. An "exhaustive search of all records and documents available" did not produce a correct list of warrants outstanding. The shortages of the three former employees were laid to inadequate and inaccurate records and controls. The auditors concluded that it was impossible to obtain a picture of the financial condition of the state or a history of financial operations from the general accounting records.[20]

A complete change in the auditor's records was recommended in the audit report:

The need for changes in method and records may be understood in a general way when consideration is given to the fact that no revision of major importance has been made during the past 25 years. Comparing the volume of state business 25 years ago with that of the present, and taking cognizance of the increased knowledge regarding accounting and governmental procedure, together with the knowledge of the imperfections of the present system, no doubt can remain that improvements amounting virtually to a complete revision of the financial and accounting methods of the state are absolutely essential.[21]

Supervision of Accounting

The 1925 law had stated that the comptroller, subject to the approval of the commission, "shall formulate and prescribe for all departments a system of uniform records, accounts, statements, estimates, vouchers, bills, and demands with suitable books of instruction covering the installation and use thereof." [22] It was further provided that the accounting system and forms so prescribed should be adopted and employed by the departments.

An attempt to make changes in the accounting records of the state auditor's office met with failure. In 1926 the comptroller introduced a machine method of keeping the general ledger in the auditor's office, but the auditor retained his hand-kept records and after a year discarded the more modern methods that the comp-

[20] Report of the examination by Hines and Bachmann, Certified Public Accountants (477 typed pages), January 16, 1928.
[21] Ibid., pp. 6–7.
[22] Session Laws, 1925, Ch. 426, Art. III, Sec. 10.

troller had set up for him.[23] A few minor suggestions made by the comptroller were accepted, but he was unable to introduce any major changes in the financial records and procedures in the state auditor's and state treasurer's offices.

Supervision over accounting in the operating departments was more effective. Comptroller Rines retained a public accountant on the commission pay roll for some time; he made surveys of the accounting practices in various departments and introduced new forms and methods where needed. Comptroller Pearlove made one of the three supervising examiners in the public examining division a "system man," who was responsible for checking accounting systems in the departments and making changes where desirable. Changes in the systems were usually accepted without question by the heads of the operating departments, who apparently welcomed this type of technical assistance.

No complete, uniform accounting system for all departments, together with a manual of instructions, was ever formulated. The difficulty of doing this without the full cooperation of the authority keeping the central proprietary accounts apparently prevented the comptrollers from even trying to carry into effect the mandate of the statutes. Probably the closest approaches to any manual of instructions or uniform system were the formulation of a uniform set of ledger sheets in 1926 and the issuance of a set of budgetary accounting instructions in 1938.

The comptroller's supervision over accounting also extended to local subdivisions of government. No uniform classification of accounts nor set of accounting records was officially promulgated for these subdivisions, but the comptroller was successful in making some changes in the systems used by individual counties and cities. One difficulty encountered in improving the accounting in the local units of government was their lack of sufficient, competent employees to operate new systems, once they were installed. This was particularly true in the counties, where the auditors were elected by popular vote; their deputies often were appointed on a political basis and the number of employees in the office was restricted by rigid provisions of state law.

[23] Hines and Bachmann cite this as evidence of the "lack of harmony between the Department of Administration and Finance and the Auditor's office" (see their report, p. 67). The comptroller's authority to prescribe the kind of records and accounts to be kept in the auditor's and treasurer's offices had been upheld by the attorney general in an opinion delivered on April 22, 1926.

COMMISSION OF ADMINISTRATION AND FINANCE

The Governor and the Audit Function

Although the legal pre-audit of payments from the treasury was in the hands of an independent official, the postaudit of financial transactions was the duty of the comptroller, appointed by and directly responsible to the governor. Although there is very little recorded evidence of the governor's part in influencing postaudits, his hand may be discerned.

The postaudit offered a convenient device for attacking the records of political enemies who had been or were in state office. In 1931 and again in 1939 changes in the political affiliations of the governor and comptroller were followed by comprehensive audits of some of the state departments still under appointees of previous governors; in several cases these audits were followed by resignations. In 1939, upon refusal of the commissioner of conservation to resign, the comptroller brought charges against him, on the basis of which the governor's office held hearings and dismissed him.[24] Other audits not only led to the prosecution of some former officials and employees but also furnished information on the mistakes of various administrations for possible use in future election campaigns.[25] Another example of the usefulness of the audit was in 1932, when an audit allegedly revealing extravagance in the administration of the highway patrol appeared during the political campaign in which the chief of the patrol, Earle Brown, was opposing the incumbent, Floyd Olson, for the office of governor.

Having the postaudit power in the hands of an official of the administration made it possible to use the power in favor of political friends.[26] Insufficient time and inadequate staff assistance, or the need of starting another audit on a particular date, often made it possible to stop certain examinations before they had gone into very much detail on the transactions of some officials. Sometimes no regular audit was even attempted; the administration of federal and state relief funds by state officials was not audited until 1939. The governor had been responsible in large measure for

[24] Charges of this nature should be distinguished from charges resulting in criminal action. No criminal action was brought against the conservation commissioner.

[25] Cf. *Inaugural Message of Governor Harold E. Stassen*, January 3, 1939, p. 15; and *Report from the Joint Senate and House Investigating Committee Covering the Acts and Activities of the Various Governmental Departments and Agencies of the State of Minnesota* (1939–40 Interim), pp. 32–35.

[26] There is no indication, however, that examiners discovered irregularities and then concealed them in the audit reports; to have done so would have been running a risk of being charged with malfeasance in office.

relief expenditures in 1933 and 1934, and his party had a majority vote on the Executive Council, which was in charge of relief administration in 1937 and 1938.

In general, however, the governor's influence did not detract from the effectiveness of the postaudit in so far as a check on receipts and cash in the departments was concerned. Significantly, too, the investigations by legislative committees, including the one in 1939, found very little irregularity in the handling of receipts. The irregularities found by investigators were almost always among the expenditures. Expenditure documents were given little attention in the postaudit because the disbursements had been subject to a prior audit by the state auditor.

Audits of local authorities also offered opportunities for carrying out the governor's will in one way or another, but there is no record that the audits were unusual in any respect because of the governor's control over the comptroller.

Chapter 7

THE PROCUREMENT FUNCTION

RECOGNITION of the advantages of centralized purchasing, particularly as a means of implementing expenditure control, had been a motivation in the passage of the reorganization act. Significantly, in the various political and legislative attacks on the Commission of Administration and Finance, no suggestions were made that purchasing should be further decentralized, and when the commission was abolished, it was in favor of a new department, with promise of greater centralization and supervision of the procurement function.

From a study of the operations of the Big Three in procurement matters, the following facts emerge: (1) The commission never fully accepted its statutory responsibility for active supervision of all purchasing; (2) centralized purchasing, even excepting institutional buying, was never achieved under the Big Three; (3) neither statute nor rules definitely assured protection against the misuse of the purchasing and printing powers; (4) the purchasing and store divisions did bring savings to the state on those items that were purchased in large quantity; and (5) the purchasing commissioner was mainly concerned with buying rather than with the broader aspects of procurement and financial administration.

Provisions for Central Supervision

Full supervision over all state procurement activities was given to the Commission of Administration and Finance by the reorganization act.

> The Commission shall have the power to supervise and control . . . the making of all contracts and the creation or incurrence of all financial or contractual obligations; the purchase, rental, or furnishing of all property, equipment, supplies, or material, and all telegraph, telephone, or lighting service; the construction and erection of all buildings and structures by or for the state. . . . [Section 3]

> The Commission . . . shall have and exercise rights and duties now by law vested in or imposed upon the Printing Commission of the state. [Section 6]

Not only was the commission responsible for general supervision over purchases, rentals, and contracts but it was also charged with the responsibility—centered in the purchasing commissioner—for centralizing the actual purchasing work in its offices, except for the procurement of institutional supplies and the purchasing for such departments as the commission might choose to place in the hands of departmental purchasing agents.

The Commission shall have the power . . . to purchase, except as otherwise herein provided, all supplies and equipment for all officials, departments, and agencies of the state government, including tools, machinery, and materials to be used by the state in the construction and maintenance of state highways. . . . [Section 4]

The Commission shall have the power . . . to procure by lease, with the approval of the governor, office space and buildings for the use of the state government or any department, office, or institution thereof. . . . [Section 4]

The Commissioner of Purchases shall have immediate supervision of all purchases and contracts made by the Commission. . . . [Section 7]

The single case in which departmental purchasing was continued by the law was the procurement of institutional supplies. In the section of the act transferring the old purchasing powers of the Board of Control to the new commission, the right was reserved for the board to continue to purchase supplies and equipment for the institutions, subject, however, to the commission's supervision.

The Commission, subject to the provisions of law governing the same, shall have and exercise all the rights and powers and perform all the duties now by law vested in or imposed upon the state board of control in relation to the erection and construction of buildings, the purchase of fuel or placing of insurance on buildings or their contents, and the purchase of supplies and materials, except that supplies, materials, furnishings and equipment to be used in or about the institutions under the control of said board, including supplies, equipment and materials for repairs to buildings under its control, shall be purchased by said board under the supervision of said commission, not including in such exception, however, supplies, equipment and materials for the erection or construction of buildings nor the purchase of fuel. . . . [Section 6]

The commission's powers were implemented by a further provision: "The Commission, subject to the approval of the governor, may make rules, regulations, and orders regulating and governing the manner and method of purchasing, delivering, and handling of, and the contracting for supplies, equipment, and other property for the various officials, departments and agencies of the state government and institutions under their control." [Section 7]

The law further set forth the subject matter that should be included in such rules.

Such rules, regulations, and orders shall be uniform, so far as practicable, shall be of general or limited application, and shall include provisions for the following:

(1) The advertisement for and the receipt of bids for supplies and other property and the stimulation of competition with regard thereto;

(2) The purchase of supplies and other property without advertisement or the receipt of bids, where the amount involved will not exceed five hundred dollars, when, in the judgment of the commissioner of purchases, it is expedient;

(3) The purchase of supplies and other property without competition, in cases of emergency requiring immediate action;

(4) The purchase of certain supplies, equipment, and other property by long or short term contracts, or by purchases or contracts made at certain seasons of the year, or by blanket contracts or orders covering the requirements of one or more departments, offices, and commissions;

(5) The time for submitting estimates for various supplies, equipment, and other property;

(6) Regulations to secure the prompt delivery of commissary and other necessary supplies;

(7) Standardization of forms for estimates, orders, and contracts;

(8) Standardization of specifications for purchasing supplies, equipment, and other property;

(9) Standardization of quality, grades, and brands to eliminate unnecessary number of commodities or of grades or brands of the same commodity;

(10) The purchase of supplies and other property locally upon permission, specific or otherwise, of the commissioner of purchases;

(11) The use and disposal of the products of state institutions;

(12) The disposal of obsolete, excess, and unsuitable supplies, salvage, waste materials, and other property, and the transfer of same to other departments, offices, and commissions;

(13) The storage of surplus supplies, equipment, and other property not needed for immediate use;

(14) The testing of commodities or supplies or samples thereof;

(15) Hearings on complaints in respect to the quality, grade, or brand of commodities or supplies;

(16) The waiver of rules in special cases. [Section 7]

Purchase of Matériel

The commission began its work without attempting to achieve centralized purchasing immediately. Motivated by lack of space and a desire to keep its pay roll down, it decided to let the separate purchasing staffs of the Highway Department and the university remain where they were — the Board of Control's purchasing staff was separate also — and, on all but the more costly or quantity items, to let other departments and agencies decide for themselves the extent to which they would use the commission's purchasing facilities. The commission later tended to do more and more of the buying for the state departments that did not have their own purchasing staffs, but some purchases were always made directly by the departments without advance authorization of the commission. The House of Representatives, friendly to the Big Three, turned over the procurement of its supplies and printing to the commission, but the Senate, still showing its hostility, refused to do more than instruct its secretary to secure prices from the Big Three before making purchases.[1] After 1928 the university was entirely exempt from the control of the Big Three. On different occasions the buyers of the Board of Control, the Highway Department, and the State Relief Agency functioned in the offices of the Big Three and under the general supervision of the purchasing commissioner,[2] but their staffs were never consolidated with that of the commission.[3] The Rural Credit Department, too, purchased independently after 1933.

More concerned with securing results in terms of economy, the first commission failed to adopt the comprehensive rules for all phases of purchasing that had been envisioned when the reorganization act was adopted. Later commissions likewise paid little attention to rule-making. Even after the attorney general had held that the law implied the necessity of certain rules in 1938, the commission merely adopted a regulation on advertising for bids, notified purchasing staffs of other departments by letter, and let rule-making go at that.

In the purchase of supplies and materials the purchasing division's usual procedure was to receive a requisition from the department wanting the goods, to secure bids informally, and to write a

[1] *St. Paul Dispatch*, December 7, 1926, January 4, 6, 1927.

[2] The Board of Control for three years up to 1931, Highway and Relief on several occasions after 1931. Only the buyers from one of these three agencies were located in the commission offices at any one time; that is, the buyers from one agency had always moved back to desks in their own department before buyers from another agency came in.

The Board of Control, exempted by express provision of the 1925 act, voluntarily agreed to merge its purchasing with that of the Big Three on July 1, 1927. The board addressed a letter to Commissioner Austin appointing him as its purchasing agent but this letter of appointment was withdrawn when Austin resigned in 1931 (*ibid.*, September 29, 1926, March 9, June 30, 1927).

[3] The buyers from the other agencies always made purchases for their agency alone; there was no attempt to route requisitions from other departments to them, nor to achieve any centralized purchasing procedures. The only "consolidation" was that the other buyers were physically present in the commission offices and subject to the supervision of the purchasing commissioner.

purchase order for the transaction. Requisition forms were furnished by the Big Three; teachers' colleges sent in their requests on special forms quarterly; all other departments and agencies filed requisitions one at a time as often as they desired. Reference to a page number in the catalog of some manufacturer or wholesale house, or sometimes a reference to a United States government standard, served to identify the item wanted; with a few exceptions the state did not take the trouble to establish standard specifications of its own. On the more important items bids were taken by telephone or by circulating an invitation to bid among possible bidders by mail; [4] on small items the procedure was very informal. Upon the purchasing commissioner's review of the bids (if they had been taken) he decided to whom the purchase orders should be written, then it was written and signed and copies sent to the vendor and the department.

Once the purchase order was written, the division's task was regarded as complete. Time of delivery, quantity actually received, testing the quality of goods, storage, invoices, and payment of bills were responsibilities of the departments themselves. [5] In later years the Big Three's appropriation was insufficient to enable it to enlarge its staff to perform these functions, even if it had tried to do so.

A very few commodities were procured on blanket contracts rather than on individual purchase orders. One of these was coal, which was bought on the basis of rigid specifications as to B.T.U., moisture, and ash content, and deliveries of which were subject to sampling and laboratory testing. Newspaper advertisement for bids preceded the letting of coal contracts each year. Electric-light bulbs were usually bought on an annual price agreement or contract, subject to a more-or-less provision as to quantity. For a number of years contracts were secured with a few gasoline companies allowing the state specified discounts from established prices. A type-

[4] In the ten months preceding the abolition of the Department of Administration and Finance, the department advertised for formal bids in a legal newspaper on all purchases amounting to $500 or more, as required by an attorney general's opinion. The opinion came as a result of the Bemidji Teachers' College project controversy, when the commission proceeded to buy material for a major construction project without taking formal bids (see Chapter 2, page 44). Until the opinion was given the commission's actions were based on the premise that advertising and formal bids were required only on formal contracts.

[5] The Highway Department maintained a testing and research laboratory of its own at the university.

writer agreement, calling for trade-ins at specified times, covered the requirements of numerous state departments.

Although it is not possible to establish what savings prevailed as a result of the purchasing division's total activities, the department was able to boast of specific economies on certain commodities.[6] In its first year of operation alone, the purchase of coal on a B.T.U. basis instead of the former run-of-the-mine basis was said to have saved $17,000.[7] That same year the price of automobile license tags was cut 20 per cent from the previous year and a discount of two cents a gallon was secured on a million gallons of gasoline. Some years later the purchasing division was still able to point to savings on certain items, including coal purchases again, repair parts for motor vehicles, tires, and inner tubes, and new typewriters.[8]

Economy was not assured by rigid regulations, however, but rested upon the ability and integrity of the purchasing division personnel. The absence of definite, publicized rules to make sure that bidding was open to all potential bidders on the basis of fair competition, and the lack of assurance that awards were made fairly and honestly to the lowest qualified bidder created doubt as to the economies resulting from state purchasing procedures, especially after 1931. A 1935 bill, which passed one house of the legislature but failed to pass the other, would have set up statutory provisions for advertising for bids (on purchases of more than $500), bidding procedures, and purchase awards, similar to the statute that regulated purchasing by local units of government. An attorney general's opinion[9] in 1938 made advertising for bids in pur-

[6] Even on specific commodities, where information is available, the question arises as to how savings should be measured — in terms of market prices, prices formerly paid for similar articles, or some other standard. No one knows what prices departments would have paid had they bought directly, and therefore the savings through central purchasing can never be determined with precision.

[7] Information as to savings in the first year was contained in Governor Christianson's keynote address in his campaign for reelection, September 28, 1926. See also Henry Rines, "The Department of Administration and Finance," *Minnesota Municipalities*, November 1928, pp. 517–19.

[8] The information is from a nine-page mimeographed brochure entitled "Advantages of a State Centralized Purchasing System," given to the legislature in 1935, when the Department of Administration and Finance was under attack from legislators. On the opposite side of the picture, the evidence was presented to a legislative investigating committee in 1935 to show that on certain items the unit prices paid by the state were considerably higher than those paid by the university. These items, however, were school and office supplies, where educational discounts usually are very substantial (*Report of Investigating Committee* [1935 Legislative Session], p. 45).

[9] See above, Chapter 2, page 44.

chases of $500 or more a necessity, and in the last ten months of the commission's existence this rule was complied with.[10]

The purchasing division's willingness to serve the departments, together with lack of a procedure for checking requisitions against central accounts of allotments and encumbrances, resulted in numerous purchases for departments in excess of approved allotments.[11]

Operation of the Central Storeroom

Office supplies in regular demand were handled through a central store. The purchasing division customarily bought various paper supplies, inks, typewriter ribbons, and several hundred other office supplies in quantity, stocked them in a central store, and sold them at retail to state departments and agencies upon their requisitions. The price to departments was ordinarily fixed at 10 per cent above the invoice cost of the goods; the margin was to cover the cost of handling, including salaries, freight, possible waste or spoilage, and other expenses.

The store had been initiated by the Board of Control, pursuant to a 1917 statutory authorization.[12] It had a capital appropriation of $10,000, and when, in 1925, it was transferred to the Commission of Administration and Finance, the volume of business averaged between $15,000 and $20,000 a year.

The commission built up the store's business until it had reached more than $50,000 a year when it was turned over to the commission's successor in 1939.[13] This was accomplished both by a substantial increase in the volume of supplies handled and by adding two services — duplicating and typewriter repair. The store began

[10] Ray P. Chase, former state auditor and Republican critic of the Farmer-Labor regime, in an article printed in the *Fairmont Daily Sentinel* on December 14, 1938, cited specific evidence to show that in May 1934 Purchasing Commissioner Erickson had approved a series of seven purchase orders for the same commodity, to be delivered to the same department, in amounts slightly under $500, all of these orders going to the same company and being paid for by one warrant.

[11] See above, Chapter 5, page 35. Apparently, state officers and employees made use of the purchasing division in the early years to procure personal articles at substantial savings. The assistant purchasing commissioner, Waddell, was discharged in 1931, when it was discovered that he had charged such orders to the state and in several instances had failed to pay for them after the purchasers had reimbursed him. This incident resulted in an order from the comptroller prohibiting the procurement of personal supplies by state employees through the purchasing division.

[12] The appropriation act (*Session Laws*, 1917, Ch. 437, Sec. 18) authorized the board to set aside $5,000 to be used as a "store revolving fund." In 1919 another $5,000 was added to it (*ibid.*, 1919, Ch. 465, Sec. 19).

[13] The information is taken from records of the store.

doing multigraphing and mimeographing for the numerous departments that did not have their own duplicating machines in 1926,
and it undertook typewriter repair service some years later. These
services never were large enough to demand the full-time work
of two men, but the employees who performed these duties also
helped in the store's major business of handling supplies.

The 10 per cent margin on prices was more than sufficient to
meet the store's pay roll and expenses, even though the assistant
purchasing commissioner and other commission employees were put
on the store pay roll part of the time in later years when the commission's appropriation was small. Instead of reducing the prices
to departments, however, prices were kept up and the resulting
profits were invested in increasing inventories, thus in effect raising
the store capitalization.[14]

The store offered a convenience to those departments whose
habits were to buy in small quantities whenever goods were needed.
On some items the store's charges to departments exceeded normal
retail prices, but on a majority of items the store was able to sell
its supplies at a figure below the normal unit cost in retail channels.

Building Contracts

Contracts for building construction and repairs were a direct
responsibility of the commission. Except for exemptions made in
appropriation acts in 1929 and 1935, the Big Three formulated and
executed contracts for state buildings, including structures at the
institutions under the Board of Control and at the state fair
grounds.[15] The executive secretary of the Big Three and the purchasing commissioner usually worked together on such matters, and
the contracts were formally approved by the commission as a whole.

Architects and engineers for the construction were chosen without bids or other competition by the commission and were paid
professional fees based on the cost of the buildings. The fees came
from the appropriations for the various buildings, not from the
appropriations of the Department of Administration and Finance.

[14] By 1939 the "surplus" exceeded $19,000. Actually the original law had not
contemplated that there would be any surplus.
[15] The State Agricultural Society, which was in charge of the state fair, had been
exempted from the operations of the reorganization act by the act itself, except that,
like county agricultural societies receiving state aid, it was subject to postaudit,
it submitted biennial budget requests, and it was subject to the supervision of the commission in erection of new buildings costing $5,000 or more (Art. VII).

COMMISSION OF ADMINISTRATION AND FINANCE

Until 1931 the commission followed the Board of Control's former practice of selecting one "state architect" and one engineering firm to handle all the construction; in that year the commission decided to distribute the work for the several buildings among several architects and engineers, and this practice was usually followed from that time on.

After the architect's plans and specifications had been approved by the proper authorities representing the agency or institution for whom the building was being erected, the commission advertised for bids for contracts.[16] This procedure followed the letter of the law.[17] Public opening and tabulation of bids was followed by awards to the lowest responsible bidders, who were required to furnish performance bonds.

As work under the contracts progressed, invoices for partial payments to the contractors were first approved by the architect, then approved by the commission, and then voucher warrants were drawn by the department for whom the building was being constructed. The voucher warrants were abstracted in the same manner as other state disbursements, routed to the budget and accounting division of the commission and then to the state auditor for his pre-audit before payment was made. Final payment was authorized by the architect and the commission only when the building was formally accepted by the state. A memorandum record of the payments on such contracts was kept in the contract file in the purchasing division.

Other Contractual Services

Highway contracts were primarily the responsibility of the Department of Highways, subject to the supervision and approval of the commission.[18] The Highway Department customarily did all

[16] Except in 1937–38, when on the Bemidji State Teachers' College project only the skilled work, such as electrical wiring, was done on contract, and the rest was done by WPA labor with materials bought by the purchasing division.

[17] The reorganization act had transferred to the commission "subject to the provisions of law governing the same" the Board of Control's duties relative to erection and construction of buildings (Art. III, Sec. 6). An older statute had stated that "The board shall not let any contract for the erection and construction of new buildings that may hereafter be constructed without first publicly advertising for at least two weeks in some legal newspaper published in the county where the work is to be performed. . . ." (*Mason's Minnesota Statutes*, 1927, Sec. 3146).

[18] The statute had given the commission supervision over all contracts, but it had directed that the commission itself should initiate and execute only certain types, such as building construction and repairs, coal, etc.

the preliminary work, including preparation of specifications, advertisement for bids, receipt and tabulation of bids, and decisions as to the contract award; the commission reviewed the tabulation of bids and approved the award; [19] then the Highway Department took care of the execution of contracts, including supervision of the work and payments on the contracts. Extras were often added to the contracts by the Highway Department after they had been let, because unforeseen conditions developed in the actual work. A special law provided for arbitration methods to be used if there was disagreement between the department and the contractor on the value of extra work done.[20]

Other contracts made by the departments were also referred to the commission for its approval. Game and fish department contracts for removal of rough fish from certain lakes, the contract for the concession at Douglas Lodge in Itasca State Park, and other similar agreements were entered into only with approval of the commission.

Leases were written by the commission for the rental of office space for state agencies in buildings in St. Paul, Minneapolis, Duluth, and other cities. These were customarily a matter of direct negotiation; no attempt was made to put them on a formal bid basis. Departments were free to rent on a month-to-month basis, however, without formal lease or supervision, until January 1, 1938, when a written rent memorandum to be initiated by the department and approved by the commission was required for all rentals of real property.[21] The use of this memorandum form tightened up the renting procedure and placed it under more control. Leases of state-owned property, such as trust-fund lands and rural credit properties, were never subject to the commission's jurisdiction.

The commission also had been given authority to supervise and

[19] In connection with a suit charging fraud and collusion in the letting of several highway paving contracts in 1932 (Chapter 2, pages 31–32), Purchasing Commissioner Erickson defended the Big Three as follows: "The Department of Administration and Finance is an administrative body. We have no technical experts or engineering department to check and scrutinize details. We do not know paving costs on the various types of work. The Highway Department has experts for this. We merely approve the award of contracts made by the Highway Department" (*St. Paul Dispatch,* May 4, 1932). Budget Commissioner Wittich and Comptroller Pearlove, in the same case, passed the buck to the purchasing commissioner, Mrs. Wittich explaining that the individual members of the commission had so many duties to perform they merely gave formal approval to each other's actions (*ibid.,* October 24, 1933).

[20] *Mason's Minnesota Statutes,* 1927, Sec. 2554, Sub. 17.

[21] Form letter issued November 15, 1937, over the budget commissioner's signature.

111

control the renting of personal property (furniture and equipment) for the use of state departments and agencies. Departments, however, ordinarily entered into informal agreements for the rent of such property without reference to the commission. The only major use of rented equipment was in the Highway Department, which at one time engaged in an extensive rental of trucks and heavy road equipment without written agreements or the commission's supervision.[22] The commission made no attempt to interfere.

Furnishing of telephone, telegraph, and lighting service also was specifically placed under the commission's supervision by law. Contracts for regulating the telephone service in the capitol buildings were written by the commission, though each department determined the amount of service it desired. One of these contracts caused difficulty with the attorney general.[23] Since telephone and telegraph rates were fixed by utility-regulating bodies, no other attempts were made to write contracts or purchase orders for such service to state offices. Lighting in the capitol buildings was furnished by the state's own power plant, and electric service to other state offices never received particular attention from the commission.[24]

Fidelity and surety bonds for state officials and employees were subject to the approval of the commission as to amount—unless the amount was fixed by statute—and the approval of the comptroller in general.[25] The type and general form of the bond were to be arranged by the comptroller, with adequate protection for the state being a primary consideration. Purchase orders were not written for such bonds, nor were bids received. Officials usually were

[22] It was on equipment rentals that several prosecutions of highway officials and contractors were based in 1939–40. Cf. *Report from the Joint Senate and House Investigation Committee Covering the Acts and Activities of the Various Governmental Departments and Agencies of the State of Minnesota* (1939 Legislative Session), pp. 1–6.

[23] See above, Chapter 2, page 35.

[24] On one occasion the purchasing commissioner reported a saving of $2,050 a year in the letting of a contract for lighting Camp Ripley, National Guard cantonment.

[25] Art. XVIII, Sec. 3 of the Reorganization Act authorized the commission to prescribe the amounts of bonds for state officials; and an older law (*Mason's Minnesota Statutes*, 1927, Sec. 9694) provided that official bonds of state officers and employees should be approved "by the governor and the public examiner, or one of them," which in effect meant approval by the comptroller alone (after 1925). Later laws (*Session Laws*, 1929, Ch. 263, and *ibid.*, 1931, Ch. 233) gave the commission further authority in deciding which state employees should be bonded and the amounts and gave the comptroller specific powers in the general approval of such bonds.

free to select their own bondsmen, but the comptroller often designated the bonding company for employees' bonds, a practice that
caused friction with departments.

Printing and Advertising

Biennial contracts for state printing were let by the Commission of Administration and Finance and actual administration of the
printing was left to the state expert printer.

The old printing law, carried over from the days before 1925,
designated certain classes of state printing and provided for letting a biennial contract for each class, after advertising for bids
on them.[26] The printing to be included in each class was defined in
the statute. The state printer prepared general specifications which
were approved by the commission and made a part of each contract. When a requisition for printing was received, the printer was
supposed to write a printing order for it to the firm whose contract
covered that class of work. Printing orders did not specify any
prices, but invoices for completed printing were submitted to the
state printer for his approval before they were paid.[27]

Theoretically the blanket-contract method of printing had the
advantage of getting low prices, because it assured successful bidders of a substantial quantity of work. The form of the contracts,
however, with separate unit prices on various items, such as different types of composition, presswork, paper stock, binding, etc.,
made it possible for a printer who was familiar with the work to
present a bid so low as to lose money on certain jobs under the
contract and yet make a good profit on other jobs in which the
elements of the work were in different proportion to each other.[28]
A greater weakness lay in the matter of extras, overtime, and vari-
ations from the contracts; the impossibility of writing contract spec-

[26] *Mason's Minnesota Statutes*, 1927, Secs. 5674, 5676, 5677. Contracts were let
annually until 1926, when they were changed to a biennial basis pursuant to a 1925
amendment of the printing law. Seven classes of printing were prescribed by statute,
but the commission had the authority to subdivide the classes further.

[27] "The State expert printer . . . shall receive and pass upon all bills for printing,
advertising and binding for the state" (*ibid.*, Sec. 5672).

[28] A committee of printers appointed to review the letting of a contract on class
3A printing in 1938, after one of the bidders had questioned whether the award had
been made to the lowest bidder, reported in part as follows: "In our opinion it is
very difficult for any printer to make an intelligent estimate under the specifications in
class 3A as they are not broken down enough to cover the numerous phases of work
required by the state" ("Minutes of the Commission," Book B, pp. 1525–26 [December
7, 1938]).

ifications to cover all the parts of many printing jobs made it possible for printing firms to add extra charges to their invoices for special typesetting, paper stock, "tipping in" inserts, and other work not specifically covered by the contract.[29]

The greatest weakness in state printing, however, was the work that the state printer let outside the contracts. This was usually placed at his discretion and at rates agreed on between the printing firm and the state printer; there was no advertising for bids nor open competition. Such printing often brought high prices, a fact that at times caused friction with the departments that had to pay the bill; other irregularities also resulted.[30] In some years as much as 50 per cent of the state printing was done outside the contracts.

Some printing never received the attention of the state printer. Printing plants at several state institutions did work, not only for their own institutions but for other institutions and for the Board of Control, outside the supervision of the state printer or the Big Three. A few departments, too, ordered some printing of a minor nature done locally without routing it through the state printer's hands.

Printing was a subject of several controversies. Restrictions on the firms who could bid on printing contracts brought a law suit in 1934, as a result of which all bids were rejected and new ones were taken. Further friction arose at times when printing firms who had contracts charged that the state printer was diverting jobs covered by their contracts to other printers. Departments, too, caused trouble, particularly in later years, when some of their printing bills were in excess of the amounts that they thought reasonable.[31]

[29] For example, bills for printing the *Legislative Manual* were sometimes almost double the amount of the original contract.

[30] *Report from the Joint Legislative Investigating Committee* (1939–40 Interim), pp. 10–12. Irregularities cited in it include excessive charges for maps, alleged exorbitant charges for a pamphlet printed by a newspaper politically friendly to the administration, and large amounts of job printing that went to a company in which the state printer's brother had an interest — all outside the contracts.

[31] For example, the 1939 investigating committee calls attention to a dispute between the Railroad and Warehouse Commission and the state printer on the amount of a bill for certain job printing (*ibid.*, pp. 11–12). The Railroad and Warehouse Commission charged that the original bill ($1,240) was more than five times higher than the amount they had paid for similar printing previously ($212).

The satisfactory situation that characterized the relations between the state printer and the members of the Big Three from 1925 to 1931 did not prevail in later years. E. Mills, who succeeded S. Y. Gordon in the printing division, was discharged in 1932, after an examination made by the comptroller's office, and his successor, J. E. Spiel-

THE PROCUREMENT FUNCTION

Advertising and publication of legal notices also was subject to the state printer's supervision. The printer decided in what newspaper such notices should be printed, within the limits of the law as to the cities or counties in which the advertisement should appear. Advertisements were billed and paid at the so-called legal rate, prescribed by statute for the publication of legal notices.[32] The printer did not attempt to take bids in an effort to get a lower rate. The volume of legal notices was not large—mostly rules of certain departments and the treasurer's annual report—until 1938–39, when many advertisements were inserted calling for bids on state purchases. Most advertising of a nonlegal character, such as display advertisements of the Tourist Bureau and the Department of Rural Credit, was arranged by the departments without supervision from the state printer.

man, seems not to have been on the best of terms with his superiors (*St. Paul Dispatch,* February 27, 1932). F. R. McGowan, who succeeded Spielman, and G. F. Etzell, who served during the closing months of the commission's existence, apparently were on fairly good terms with the commission, especially the latter.

[32] *Mason's Minnesota Statutes,* 1927, Secs. 10938, 10939, and 10939–1. There was no specific statutory authority allowing payment at other than the legal rate, though various municipalities took bids for publication of their legal proceedings and paid less than the legal rate.

Chapter 8

PERSONNEL PROBLEMS

A SUBSTANTIAL portion of the Big Three's activities was centered on problems of personnel. Some of the difficulties that eventually led to the abolition of the commission had their roots in the handling of problems pertaining to state employment.

Pertinent facts with reference to the commission's powers and functioning with respect to personnel include the following: (1) The powers granted the commission relative to personnel were designed primarily to aid in controlling expenditures; (2) no adequate, comprehensive classification and compensation plan was ever put into practice; (3) making the personnel division a patronage center when applications for state employment became numerous threw the office into politics and diverted attention from its primary purpose; and (4) the personnel responsibilities that were carried out made the office unpopular with both department heads and with state employees.

Limited Powers of the Commission

The reorganization act had given the commission very few powers or duties with respect to personnel. The recommendations of the Interim Committee for a merit system in the state civil service had not been given serious consideration by the 1925 legislature.

The reorganization act provided that the commission should designate one of its members to serve as director of personnel and it limited the commission's personnel powers to five: [1]

1. To determine classes, grades, and titles of state employees, except for employees of the Board of Control and institutions under the board, deputies of elective officials, and assistant attorneys general;

2. To fix the salary scales for the various classes, grades, and titles of the state employees whose positions were subject to the commission's classification, and to require their salaries to be in conformity with the scales so established;

3. To require a complete record of the officers, assistants, and

[1] In addition the commission derived further power over personnel in connection with the operation of the budget and pre-audit functions.

116

employees appointed and employed by all state departments, officials, and agencies;

4. To require all persons lawfully appointed to state employment to answer a questionnaire as to sex, age, health, habits, character, and other qualifications requisite to the performance of their duties;

5. To transfer employees temporarily from one department or service to another when necessary to expedite the work of any department or agency.

In addition to these specific statutory powers and others implied from them, such as regulating hours, leaves of absence, and vacations, the commission acquired certain extralegal responsibilities from time to time, including an active part in the recruitment of personnel, and interest in the removal of employees, and a hand in the conduct of employee-employer relations.

The budget commissioner was designated as director of personnel, except for part of the year 1931 when the comptroller held that additional title. From 1925 to 1932 personnel work was under the active direction of an employee, usually designated as assistant director of personnel, and the commissioner did not engage in detailed personnel work himself. From 1933 to 1939 the budget commissioner took over the active direction of the division.[2] The number of employees in the personnel division was usually from two to four, except during 1939, when the division temporarily was much enlarged.

Classification and Compensation, the 1927 Plan

The first commission read the reorganization act, especially in the light of the legislative debate on it, as primarily an economy measure. The act gave the commission a large number of responsibilities, including a definite authorization to survey the organization, administration, and management of state departments, as well as the five personnel powers enumerated above. These powers it interpreted as important instruments for economy, and so one of the Big Three's earliest moves was to set in progress a survey of departments under the direction of an assistant director of personnel, to which position Mr. George Hayes was appointed. If there had been any doubts that the survey would be followed by

---

[2] At least two of the three commissioners during this period apparently were appointed more for the personnel work than for handling the budget.

117

a classification and compensation plan, these doubts were resolved by the Supreme Court decision in December 1925 holding the adoption of such a plan to be a prerequisite to salary control by the commission.[3]

The entire field work for the classification was done by three employees. Questionnaires pertaining to duties, observations of employees at work, studies of employee qualifications, consultations with department heads, and a study of salaries in other jurisdictions and in private business preceded the formulation of the compensation and classification plans. After nearly two years of work the plans were announced in the spring of 1927 and made effective on July 1 of that year.

The classification did not take into account the difference between classifying positions and allocating employees to given positions. It was a classification of employees, not positions. The commission frankly said, "Two employees may be working at the same class and grade of work and one may accomplish far in excess of the other and be creating a higher rate position than his co-worker."[4] Seven major divisions, twenty-eight classes, and one hundred and thirty-six grades were established. Schedules applying the classification plan to particular departments were issued. No effort was made to establish either uniform titles or descriptions of duties. From four to five thousand employees were affected by the plan.

Instead of providing minimum and maximum salaries with step rates in between as in modern salary schedules, the compensation plan was limited to the designation of maximum salaries for each class and grade. The plan conformed to the economy conception of the reorganization act by providing a means of holding salaries down to given maximums. Natural opposition to the plan arose among employees whose present salaries were found to be excessive and employees whose opportunities for salary increases in the future would be restricted by the necessity of securing approval of the Big Three in addition to the approval of their department heads. Adoption of the scales brought nearly four hundred reductions in salary and five hundred salary increases.[5]

[3] State ex rel. Thomas Yapp *et al.* v. Ray P. Chase *et al.*, 165 Minn. 268 (1925).
[4] From typewritten explanatory material that the commission circulated to departments with the classification plan.
[5] This information is taken from Violet Johnson, "A Survey of the Administration of the State Government in Minnesota," an unpublished thesis in the University of

For about a year the provisions of the new classification and compensation plan were carefully observed by the various departments. Continuous adjustments were made, however, necessitating the issuance of new personnel orders affecting the classification and compensation schedules as they applied to various departments. It became the custom for the maximum salary rates to be the only rates in effect. Even on that basis, however, departments found it possible to establish salaries outside of the plan, either by failing to notify the Big Three of their action or by securing the commission's approval to have a particular position designated "not within classification while position is held by present incumbent." [6] By 1930 the classification and compensation plan had become virtually a dead letter.

Classification and Compensation, 1934 and After

A second classification and compensation plan was prepared in 1934. The same procedures were again followed—employee questionnaires, supervisor questionnaires, observation of work, consultation with department heads, study of existing salaries, and study of salaries elsewhere.

By this time the personnel division's interests no longer centered on strict economy, and its knowledge of modern methods of public personnel administration had grown. The positions covered by the plan were grouped into four broad occupational "services," and within these services positions were arranged into groups, series, and classes, following in general the accepted authorities on classification. Uniform titles were established, and a statement of the duties, the exact degree of supervision involved, and typical tasks were developed for each title.[7] Two salary lists were prepared, one setting forth the range of salaries actually being paid, and one establishing new salary scales with minimum, intermediate, and maximum rates

Minnesota Library, 1929. See also a publication entitled "Personnel Survey of State of Minnesota" by the Commission of Administration and Finance, July 1, 1928, and typewritten regulations governing personnel, issued September 11, 1929. The latter emphasizes that departments are not required to pay the maximum salary allowed in the schedules and provides that the entrance salary rates of new or promoted employees should be at a lower rate for the period necessary to become familiar with the work.

[6] The wording is that used in materials issued by the commission.

[7] *Classes, Grades, and Titles of State Employees* (with class specifications), 1935. In the absence of power to prescribe entrance qualifications for employees the class specifications necessarily omitted any reference to minimum requirements for employment.

for all positions in the classification.[8] The personnel director announced that the proposed compensation plan was designed on the equitable basis of "like pay for like work under like conditions," and that prevailing salary scales in Minnesota industry and commerce had been given careful consideration in leveling out existing inequalities.[9]

The new classification theoretically went into effect January 1, 1935. The new compensation plan was to go into effect at the same time with regard to new appointments, but the commission frankly declared that it would not be necessary to put the new compensation plan into effect immediately with respect to incumbent employees.[10] The 1935 budget document contained a list of employees, present salaries, and proposed salary limits for many state departments; some employees, who saw in the plan a restraining influence upon their future salaries, effectively lobbied against it. During the 1935 legislative session the revelations of a Senate investigating committee relative to patronage practices served to discredit the personnel division among legislators.[11] The plan was said to involve an excessive increase in the cost of personal services to the state.[12] When the departmental appropriation bill was passed near the end of the session, it contained a provision, reading:

> The various state department heads shall determine the salaries to be paid to all their employees as hereinbefore provided, and any classification

[8] Both the classification and compensation plans omitted positions under the jurisdiction of the Board of Control and certain professional positions, such as instructional staffs at the state teachers' colleges.

[9] *Salary Scales for State Employes. Proposed by the Commission of Administration and Finance, Division of Personnel, and Recommended in the Biennial Budget, 1935–37* (January 1935), p. 3.

[10] "It is not mandatory that the new salary scale shown is put into immediate effect and it is the intent that where the existing salaries for the employees enumerated are either above or below the new scale, same can remain in effect until a readjustment can be made by you. Such readjustments are possible through change in duties and titles, vacancies, abolishing of a position, or change in salary. The commission will, however, expect your full cooperation in bringing all salaries in line with the new scale as ordered just as quickly as possible" (Form letter M30 to all department heads, signed by I. C. Strout, director of personnel, December 20, 1934). See also formal commission order making the classification and compensation plan effective as of January 1, 1935, signed by E. J. Pearlove, the chairman, and dated December 26, 1934.

[11] *Report of the Investigating Committee of the Senate* (1935 Legislative Session), pp. 38–40.

[12] Actually, the estimated increase of approximately 10 per cent in the salary appropriations for departments and agencies under Big Three control was due to the decision of the commission to base the compensation plan upon so-called normal or pre-depression salary levels. Cf. below, pages 122–23.

of state employees which may have been or shall be made shall not apply, any law to the contrary notwithstanding.[13]

This nullified the extensive work that had been done on the classification and compensation plan, and so the plan never went into effect. At the end of the biennium 1935–37 the restrictions imposed by the legislature upon the powers of the commission to classify employees and to fix salary scales automatically expired and they were not renewed. No attempt was made, however, to resurrect the classification and compensation plan during the remainder of the commission's life. Several departments, notably the Highway Department, made use of the 1935 classification on their own initiative. Once in 1937–38 the governor's office announced that the Commission of Administration and Finance would make a new employee classification, but nothing more was heard of it.

Personnel Records

Although the commission had no authority to determine minimum qualifications for entrance into state employment, it was required by law to secure from each person appointed to a state position information on his qualifications for the job. A questionnaire file was set up after the 1927 classification plan was established, and it may be inferred that the commission planned to use the questionnaires in assigning new employees to particular classes and grades. Department heads were expected to get the questionnaires from the newly appointed employees and forward them to the personnel division;[14] sometimes this was done, sometimes not;[15] and in the later years of the commission's history the questionnaire was often omitted because the employee already had filed some of the same information on an application-for-employment blank.

Form 303[16] was devised to enable department heads to inform the personnel division of appointments to positions and separations

[13] *Session Laws,* 1935, Ch. 391, Sec. 37.

[14] Apparently no specific provisions were made to secure similar information concerning employees already in the state service.

[15] Incompleteness of the questionnaire file as a source of information on employees was revealed upon establishment of the State Employees' Retirement Association in 1929. The legislature directed the Commission of Administration and Finance to give the new retirement association a list of employees, their ages, length of service, and a few other facts, all of which should have been available from the questionnaires. The commission found it necessary to circularize all departments with a special blank to get the necessary information.

[16] The accounting forms started numbering with 100, the purchasing forms with 200, the personnel forms with 300, etc.

from the service and to request adjustments in salary, class, and grade.[17] First used only for changes in the permanent pay roll, the form later was used for temporary appointments also, and it became one of the commission's most effective means of control over departments. The form provided a space for noting the commission's action upon the request of the department, and commission approval of the necessary forms 303 was made a prerequisite to pay-roll changes. Most forms were approved; some, especially those requesting salary adjustments, were disallowed. On numerous occasions, especially after 1931, the personnel division rejected large numbers of 303's proposing wholesale salary increases for state employees.[18]

Earnings records were established by the personnel division in the fiscal year 1931–32. Up to that time, permanent pay rolls were checked against the commission's established salary schedules for each department; temporary and special pay rolls (which at times may have included additional compensation for permanent employees) were not checked. From 1932 to 1939, however, separate earnings records were kept and posted by hand for all permanent and temporary employees, except employees of state institutions, the university, the State Relief Agency, and the hourly workers of the Highway Department. The records were kept by a pay-roll clerk, across whose desk were routed pay-roll voucher warrants (before they were released) and approved forms 303. This clerk, therefore, not only recorded earnings but was the focal point for the pre-audit control of personal service expenditures.[19]

Because the Commission of Administration and Finance kept the employees' earnings records and pre-audited pay-roll disbursements the task of enforcing pay cuts fell to it. The "payless vacation" plan of 1932, accomplished by executive request, was followed by reduced appropriations passed by the 1933 legislature, looking toward a possible 20 per cent reduction in salaries of more than $1,200

[17] The form, entitled "Application for Adjustment of Personnel," was initiated in order to provide a means by which a department could secure a change in one of the commission's salary schedules. Following adoption of the 1927 classification, the commission, by a series of formal orders, established separate schedules of permanent positions and salaries (in line with the plan as a whole) for each department.

[18] The peak was reached in May 1936, when six hundred requests for increases were rejected.

[19] Mrs. Wittich, director of personnel, who was responsible for initiating this new system of salary control, made a special report to Governor Olson in March 1932 on personnel conditions and practices in the departments, in which she pointed out various irregularities resulting from the former inadequate records and control.

as a means of holding expenditures as close as possible to the state's income.[20] The salary reduction was not mandatory, however;[21] some employees were cut 20 per cent; in other departments savings in other items were effected and the salary cut was only 5 or 10 per cent; in the departments operating on reappropriated receipts there were few, if any, wage reductions. Employees who suffered salary reductions tended to blame the Big Three, who really were not responsible. The 1935 legislature provided a 10 per cent mandatory salary reduction for positions in all departments with a compensation of $3,000 or more, and a 10 per cent permissive reduction for salaries between $1,320 and $3,000 for the biennium 1935–37.[22] Since the act was based on salaries as of June 1933, it fell to the lot of the Commission of Administration and Finance, who had the earnings records, to enforce this unpopular act.

Pay-roll certifications were used in 1932, 1933, and 1935–39 to compile regular monthly statistics on the number of employees and the amount of salaries paid by all departments and institutions. These certifications were executed on a personnel division form, signed by the proper department heads, and sent to the commission offices with each pay roll. The certifications, like other personnel records, indicated not where an employee was working but on what pay roll he was paid. The transfer power of the commission was sometimes used to justify the practice of having an employee work in one division or department and be paid by another.[23]

Recruitment and Removal

The reorganization act had given the Commission of Administration and Finance no power over the recruitment or removal of state employees, except employees of the commission and of the hotel inspection division.[24] With the exception of certain inspectional positions in the Department of Dairy and Food and the oil inspection division of the Department of Labor and Industry, for which examinations were required, the choice of state employees was left

[20] *Session Laws,* 1933, Ch. 413, Sec. 37.
[21] Opinion of the attorney general, June 2, 1933.
[22] *Session Laws,* 1935, Ch. 391, Sec. 37.
[23] The commission, in a typewritten report covering its activities for the first five years (1925–30), made reference to its power to effect temporary transfers of employees from department to department, and recommended that they be given authority to make permanent transfers.
[24] *Session Laws,* 1925, Ch. 426, Art. XII, Sec. 2. For an example of the commission's control over the personnel of this division, see *St. Paul Dispatch,* October 18, 1929.

solely to the various department heads, and the right of removal also was unlimited except for these positions.[25] Nevertheless, some supervision over recruitment and removal came to be included among the activities of the department. A discussion of these activities rather naturally falls into five periods, representing the terms of the five budget (personnel) commissioners.

From 1925 to 1931 questions related to recruitment and removal did not demand much attention from the personnel division. Vacancies were filled directly by the appointing authorities. Sometimes they appointed friends or relatives or used an appointment to pay a political debt; at other times the appointing authority made a selection from the applicants who had filed an application for employment with him. In some cases department heads notified a private business school when there were clerical vacancies and the school would refer a suitable candidate to the department. It is recorded that at least one department often went to the St. Paul YWCA employment office, and occasional use was made of private commercial employment agencies.[26] Toward the end of this period a change occurred, as a result of the beginning of the economic depression. Existence of a personnel division in the offices of the Big Three naturally attracted candidates for employment (who were probably unaware of the statutory limitations upon the powers of the personnel division) and the personnel division began to receive and file applications for work.

From 1931 to 1933 private employment continued to decline, and this, coupled with the change in state administration, brought many insistent demands for state jobs. Until the summer of 1932 an assistant director of personnel interviewed applicants and used personal influence to find places for some of them. In the following year applications were received and interviews conducted primarily by clerks in the budget commissioner's office. Most persons who

[25] *Session Laws*, 1921, Ch. 495, Sec. 74; *ibid.*, 1923, Ch. 367, Sec. 2; *Mason's Minnesota Statutes*, 1927, Secs. 53–38 and 3861. A district court decision in 1932 held that the reorganization act of 1925 in effect repealed the civil service provisions governing removals of dairy and food and oil inspectors (*St. Paul Dispatch*, March 21, 1932). See also State ex rel. William H. Kinler v. Henry Rines, 185 Minn. 49, 239 N.W. 670 (1931). The Veterans' Preference Act, of course, placed some limitations upon department heads in appointments and removals (*Mason's Minnesota Statutes*, 1927, Sec. 4368–69).

[26] John Henry Thurston, "Personnel Administration in the State Government of Minnesota," an unpublished thesis in the University of Minnesota Library, 1932, pp. 125–30.

received employment, however, had applied directly to the various department heads or used fortunate political contacts. The clamor of Farmer-Labor supporters for employment of party members and for removal of "hold-over" employees continued unabated and increased after the 1932 election.[27]

Attempted centralization of hiring and an effort to bring order and system into the handling of political patronage characterized the 1933–35 period. Departments were informed that the personnel division had "developed an extra preferred and regular preferred list of the applicants on the basis of their being deserving of consideration," and that "we are now in a position to be of real service to you in the filling of vacancies." [28] Control over pay rolls and use of Form 303 gave the personnel division leverage to enforce hiring on the basis of referrals from the list of approved applicants. At the same time applicants were told to secure the proper endorsements from the local and county committees of the Farmer-Labor party.[29] A check was made of hold-over state employees to see where vacancies might be created. These policies met with disfavor among Governor Olson's all-party backers; as a result employment was slightly decentralized in 1934, with the appointment of a separate personnel director for the Highway Department, who was to be a part of the Highway Department organization.[30]

During the period 1935 through 1938 the personnel division continued to be primarily an office for receiving applications for employment and for finding jobs for as many deserving persons as possible, but the endorsement feature previously used was less important. Job placement proceeded at a moderate rate until 1937, when the pressure for placements increased, even though after six

[27] Mrs. Wittich, budget commissioner and director of personnel during this difficult period, prepared a series of form letters to be sent to job applicants and persons endorsing such applicants. In these letters she repeatedly emphasized her lack of power relative to appointments and urged direct application to department heads.

[28] Form letter M6, addressed "to all department heads," dated August 15, 1933, and signed by Commissioner I. C. Strout. This effort to centralize personnel activity in the Big Three was undertaken in spite of opinions of the attorney general on May 10 and July 31, 1933, unequivocally upholding the power of the Industrial Commission and the commissioner of highways to appoint, promote, and remove employees without the approval of the Big Three.

[29] A mimeographed form to be used in securing such endorsements was furnished by the personnel division.

[30] Apparently this move did not diminish the use of highway jobs for party patronage purposes, if one may judge from the reported testimony of Mr. J. A. Poirier, personnel director in the Highway Department, to the Senate Investigating Committee in 1935 (p. 23).

full years of control by one party the possible vacancies were growing less and less. The problem was partially solved by the creation of additional positions. On three occasions during these years the budget commissioner recommended the establishment of a merit system under a state civil service commission. In 1937 an act was passed reorganizing the Department of Conservation and directing the commissioner in charge of the department to establish a merit system governing the employment, promotion, and discharge of all employees of the department and its several divisions except the directors of the divisions and the deputies of the commissioner and the director. A trained personnel officer was appointed in July 1937 to administer this departmental merit system under the supervision of the commissioner of conservation.[31]

The five months of 1939 that preceded the abolition of the Commission of Administration and Finance marked a great increase in recruitment and removal activities. The employment center that had been set up in downtown St. Paul to handle the thousands of Republican applications for state employment between the election and the inauguration was moved into the Big Three offices. Pressure from job-seekers was particularly heavy because the passage of a civil service law gave a very considerable advantage to persons on the state pay roll as of August 1. During 1939 the recruitment and removal function demanded so much attention that the personnel division staff was increased from the four positions that had been customary in the past to a total of approximately thirty-five employees by June.[32]

The recruitment and removal function was an extralegal one; it diverted time and a portion of the appropriation away from other duties of the Big Three; it often made the personnel director unpopular with the department heads; and the process of making places for applicants often ran exactly contrary to the aims and purposes of the budget division in keeping down state expenditures. In one respect, however, this work conformed to the general purposes of the Big Three: While performing this function the Department of Administration and Finance was certainly a staff agency of the governor, responsive to his policies and direction.

[31] *Session Laws,* 1937, Ch. 310, Sec. 1e; *Minnesota Leader,* July 24, 1937, p. 6.
[32] Pay-roll abstracts of the Department of Administration and Finance for June 1939, copies of which are on file in the state auditors' office and in the Department of Administration.

PERSONNEL PROBLEMS

General Employee Relations

In the early years of the commission's history the problems arising out of employer-employee relations were usually settled by the several departments. Comparatively few serious questions were raised. After 1931, however, the Commission of Administration and Finance entered the picture, both because it could bring uniformity out of diverse departmental procedures and because it took a more active part in supervising departmental personnel matters. Thus it became natural for certain questions to be taken to the personnel division for settlement. Political activity of employees and relations with employee unions were the main problem areas of employee relationships.

The only direct limitation placed upon the political activities of state employees by the Commission of Administration and Finance was an order during the administration of Governor Olson that employees who were candidates for public office should not appear on state pay rolls.[33] The instructions made it necessary for candidates who received nominations for offices to resign or take a leave of absence without pay between the primary and the general elections. At least on one occasion the director of personnel took an active part in influencing state employees to participate in politics. The county highway foremen, appointed by direction of the personnel director in 1934, were urged to do political work within their respective areas.[34] State employees who had been active in politics before accepting appointment to their positions were not required to give up political activity at any time during the whole period from 1925 to 1939.

State employee unions grew up in the thirties, and eventually some of them took a cue from the general labor movement and asked for recognition as the sole bargaining agent for state employees in particular departments.[35] Several department heads at-

[33] Executive order dated April 21, 1932. See also form letter dated July 12, 1934, signed by I. C. Strout, personnel director. A similar order was in effect in 1936.

[34] Letter signed by I. C. Strout (See above, Chapter 2, page 36).

[35] This placed a liberal, labor administration in a difficult position. It was honor-bound to encourage union activity and yet, as the employer in the case, it did not want to take dictation from its employees. A further complication was the fact that appropriations placed limits on salaries, and appropriations were determined by legislative action, not by the administration.

An anti-administration newspaper carried an editorial in 1932 under the caption "The Greedy Partner" in which it referred to a State Federation of Labor resolution demanding that the Big Three be empowered to specify a wage scale for skilled workers on highway and bridge contracts no lower than the highest prevailing pay in private

127

tempted to deal with the unions, but finally the whole matter was referred to the director of personnel and the commission. In answer the Big Three agreed that state employees should have the right to bargain collectively with their department heads but that agreements made must not conflict with the regulations of the Big Three, with appropriation totals, or with provisions of law. It recommended that state employees who were union members submit their grievances through union representatives, but it also reserved to every employee the right to make known his grievances personally and to negotiate with his department head personally.[36] Neither the commission nor the personnel director signed any agreement with the unions. Thus the administration gave the unions the appearance of recognition but reserved to itself the power to act in specific cases.

On the matter of salaries the Big Three made two important concessions to the unions. The craft unions, which included among their members a few skilled employees of the capitol custodian, won for these employees the same salaries they were demanding in private industry.[37] Since these carpenters, plumbers, and similar employees were on full-time, year-round employment, it gave them an annual wage somewhat in excess of the average annual earnings of their fellow craftsmen in private employment. The second important victory for the unions came in 1938, when the instructions for submitting biennial budget requests recommended "that salary schedules be established after reference to scales recommended by organized labor."[38] A labor administration could do no less.

The Commission of Administration and Finance was used as the medium through which the governor regulated hours of employment and vacation periods in the last few years. Before that time announcements of administration policy on such matters were usually made directly by the governor's office.[39]

A mimeographed handbook of information on state employment

employment, as illustrating "the insatiable appetite of the labor partner in the Farmer-Labor party" (*St. Paul Dispatch*, August 18, 1932).

[36] *Ibid.*, December 27, 1937.

[37] This salary increase was made in the absence of an appropriation and necessitated a deficiency appropriation at the next legislative session.

[38] "Budget Handbook," 1938, p. 4, item 7.

[39] The first commission, in a typewritten report covering its activities from July 1, 1925, to June 30, 1930, recommended that legislation be passed authorizing the Executive Council to establish uniform rules governing hours of work, vacations, and sick leave.

PERSONNEL PROBLEMS

was published by the personnel director on January 1, 1938. In it were gathered information, regulations, and statutory provisions governing working conditions, salaries, leaves of absence, policies with respect to unions, and similar subjects. It was the first and only effort to compile such a handbook until the publication of civil service regulations in 1940.

Chapter 9

MISCELLANEOUS ACTIVITIES AND SERVICES

THE 1925 reorganization act was not conceived as the last word on the subject by the Interim Committee that prepared the bill; provision was made for further study and recommendations for changes in the state's administrative structure. Instead of expecting the busy legislative Civil Administration committees or occasional interim committees to make such studies, however, the framers of the reorganization act provided for the Commission of Administration and Finance to be, among other things, a permanent committee to study the administration and management of the state government and to make recommendations for changes that would bring further economy and efficiency. Several other duties of the commission also are discussed in this chapter.

Significant to the subjects here discussed are the following facts: (1) The commission did not attempt to use all the authority given it by statute; (2) even the partial use of its powers brought friction with the other departments; (3) the legislature was not responsive to recommendations or requests of the commission concerning reorganization, appropriations to aid property control, and the establishment of a central mailing station; and (4) despite these handicaps the commission was able to achieve some success in its miscellaneous duties.

General Surveys of Administration

The commission's responsibilities included:

The power to examine, investigate, or make a survey of the organization, administration, and management of the various departments and agencies of state government and the institutions under their control, to the end that greater efficiency and economy may be secured, better organization, reorganization, or consolidation of departments or functions effected, and all duplication of function, effort, or activity, so far as possible, eliminated. . . . The commission shall recommend to the Legislature such changes in the laws of the state as it may deem necessary, if any, as a result of any such survey or investigation or otherwise in order to secure a better organization of the state government or greater efficiency or economy in administration.[1]

[1] Art. III, Sec. 3. In order to implement this power this section of the law also gave the commission the power "for this purpose to hold hearings and prescribe rules and regulations for the conduct thereof, issue subpoenas for and compel the attend-

There is no record that the commission conducted any formal surveys, with hearings, witnesses, and the introduction of evidence. But informal surveys and studies were made by one or more commissioners on several occasions, particularly in connection with accounting and personnel work (in the early years), auditing (in the middle years), and budgeting (in the later years). The amount of written data actually assembled in support of proposals for changes in the state's administrative structure was apparently very small, but the commissioners did study the subject.

On the basis of such studies two lines of action were open to the commission and the governor: They could make such changes as were possible within the framework of existing departmental organization set up by the statutes, and they could recommend to the legislature changes in the laws, in order to effect desired reorganizations. There was no administrative authority to consolidate departments, but the governor had been given the power to appoint a person who already held one state office to another position, in addition to the first one, so long as the positions were not incompatible.[2] The commission also had the specific power to require hotel inspectors of the Department of Health to inspect food products for the Departments of Dairy and Food and of Agriculture, a power that was not used.[3]

The governor used his power to appoint a person already holding one position to take over the duties of another position on only two important occasions during the period 1925–39. In 1925 the governor appointed one person to be both commissioner of agriculture and commissioner of dairy and food,[4] and four years later the legislature authorized the consolidation of the two departments by appropriate changes in the statutes.[5] In 1939 one man was made

ance of witnesses and giving of testimony, and production of books, records, accounts, documents, and papers. . . ." Enforcement of this power was provided in a statutory requirement that "any judge of the district court in any county of the state, on application of the Commission, shall compel obedience by attachment proceedings as for contempt, as in the case of disobedience of a similar order or subpoena issued by such court. . . . "

[2] *Session Laws*, 1925, Ch. 353. Apparently the introduction and passage of this statute was to some extent a concession to the advocates of a more thorough plan of departmental consolidation.

[3] Art. IX, Sec. 2 of the reorganization act.

[4] The Interim Committee's plan had recommended the consolidation of these departments and some others into one new Department of Agriculture, but the reorganization bill as it was finally adopted provided for separate departments (Arts. VI and VII).

[5] *Session Laws*, 1929, Ch. 387.

both the superintendent of the bureau of criminal apprehension, by appointment of the governor, and the chief of the highway patrol, by appointment of the highway commissioner. Both the 1925 and 1939 dual appointments were made in advance of recommendations by the Big Three, though the commission supported them, and in the first instance it later recommended that the consolidation be made permanent by appropriate changes in the laws.

Alterations in the administrative organization, through changes in the laws, were recommended by members of the Big Three on several occasions. In 1927 Comptroller Rines recommended consolidating the Department of Dairy and Food with the Department of Agriculture, abolishing the Board of Visitors, consolidating two agencies administering soldiers' relief and soldiers' welfare, and three changes in procedures of financial administration. The Civil Administration committees of the legislature were not friendly to suggestions coming from an administrative official, and none of the proposals was passed in that year. Two years later the first two recommendations were adopted.[6]

In a report made to the governor in 1930 and covering five years of the commission's operation the Big Three recommended legislation to consolidate war veterans' activities in one department, to place livestock sanitation work under the Department of Agriculture, to establish a central office force for the examining boards, to organize a new Department of Conservation, to abolish the office of surveyor general, and to consolidate the Board of Education and the State Teachers' College Board. They also recommended changes in the laws to consolidate state purchasing, to authorize the Executive Council to transfer unexpended and unrequired appropriation balances between departments on the recommendation of the Big Three, to authorize the commission to make permanent transfers of employees between departments, and to allow the Executive Council to establish rules on office hours and employee leaves. The only suggestion adopted at the next legislative session was the one for a new Department of Conservation, which was also one of the major recommendations of the new governor.[7]

[6] *Ibid.* provided for a Department of Agriculture, Dairy, and Food; *ibid.*, Chs. 268, 273, and 274, abolished the Board of Visitors. Governor Christianson also had advocated these changes in his inaugural messages of 1927 (pp. 15–16) and 1929 (p. 12). He further recommended in 1929 a consolidation of agencies relating to the administration of the public domain into one department directed by a commissioner.

[7] *Inaugural Message of Governor Floyd B. Olson,* 1931, pp. 6–7, and *Session Laws,* 1931, Ch. 186.

132

MISCELLANEOUS ACTIVITIES

During the 1933 legislative session Comptroller Pearlove recommended transfer of the motor vehicle division from the jurisdiction of the elective secretary of state to the appointive commissioner of highways, but no change was made. In 1937 Budget Commissioner Rasmussen gave vigorous support to a proposal for the consolidation of veterans' activities in one department; a typewritten report was prepared showing appropriations, receipts, and expenditures for such purposes over a period of years, and making a comparison of the various laws under which five different agencies were extending relief or other special services to veterans. In addition to this proposal Governor Benson also urged in his inaugural message the consolidation of welfare activities in a Department of Public Welfare and the substitution of a single commissioner for the five-member commission in charge of the Department of Conservation.[8]

Again in the 1939 budget Rasmussen repeated his recommendation for a veterans' agency, and added recommendations for a new Department of Public Welfare, for a Department of Registration to handle the office work of the examining boards, and for the integration of state activities dealing with taxation and agriculture into departments. Several of these changes were also a part of the new governor's program and the legislature wrote them into the reorganization act of that year.[9]

Several facts are significant in the commission's recommendations for reorganization: First, most of the recommendations were similar to suggestions made by earlier commissions or interim committees.[10] Second, the legislature had not been cordial to the commission's recommendations and the only times that they adopted them promptly were when a new governor was making the same recommendations as the outgoing commissioners. Third, although the governors advocated similar changes in their inaugural messages, only in the case of Governor Christianson does it appear that the chief executive based his proposals upon the studies and recommendations of the Big Three. Fourth, recommendations for

[8] *Inaugural Message of Governor Elmer A. Benson,* 1937, pp. 20, 23.
[9] *Inaugural Message of Governor Harold E. Stassen,* 1939, and *Session Laws,* 1939, Ch. 431. Some consolidation of veterans' activities was provided under the adjutant general, a new Department of Social Security was created, and the Department of Taxation was reorganized.
[10] Several even resemble suggestions made by the Efficiency and Economy Commission of 1913; some of the others had been advanced by the 1925 interim committee.

removing certain responsibilities from some officials and for abolishing certain positions were another source of friction between the commission and other state officials.

Property Control

The commission had been given both the power "to supervise and control . . . the sale, disposition, use, or storage of all property belonging to the state," and the authority "at any time to examine . . . the use or disposition of state property" (Article III, Section 3). This grant of power was a natural complement to its other duties. Intelligent budgeting for new equipment would demand information on the property already on hand, its status, and use. Purchases of new property might properly be accompanied by a sale or trade-in of the old. A complete audit of financial affairs and transactions of the various state departments would naturally include a physical inventory of property as well as other assets.

Neither a perpetual inventory system nor any other procedure relating to property control was set up by the commission. The need for such an inventory was recognized several times, however. From 1931 to 1933 the budget commissioner, noting the lack of information on state-owned property, made some memoranda for her own use in connection with budget allotment requests for the purchase of property. The 1936 biennial budget estimate blanks called for departments to give information for an inventory of property; very few departments were able to furnish any information, and it was revealed that most departments did not even have a written record of their own property.[11] In the 1937 and 1939 budget documents the budget commissioner recommended the establishment of a perpetual inventory system, and he opened negotiations for a federal WPA project to help establish the original records for such a system.[12] The 1939 legislature granted a small appropriation for this purpose to the new commissioner of administration.[13]

The commission's only real attempt at property control dealt with state-owned motor vehicles. Numerous departments had cars and trucks owned by the state and operated by department officials and employees at state expense. To help prevent abuse in the

[11] Statement in *Sixth Biennial Budget*, 1937–39, p. 14.
[12] *Ibid.*, and *Seventh Biennial Budget*, 1939–41, pp. 18 and 66.
[13] *Session Laws*, 1939, Ch. 422, Sec. 18, item 6 ($12,000 for two years).

use of such vehicles the commission made a study of such cars and attempted some regulation in 1937, and early in 1938 the budget commissioner devised a form for reports on the daily use and expense of such vehicles and required departments to file such reports with him once a month.

Difficulties followed these moves.[14] The three elective railroad and warehouse commissioners, each of whom drove a state-owned car, balked at reporting their use of the cars, and they, together with the governor and some other officials, were exempted by informal agreement from the requirements. The Highway Department, which was operating many state-owned cars under ordinary licenses instead of tax-exempt plates, protested. Highway employees in the upper salary brackets, whose state-owned cars the commission ordered put in a "pool" for use when needed instead of being exclusively available to certain employees, were opposed to the commission's intervention in the matter. Some other department officials and employees, who had been collecting garage rent from the state for housing their state-owned cars at their residences, were disappointed when the commission directed that such payments be discontinued, and attempted to restrict the use of state cars for trips to and from employees' homes. Some compromises resulted but the commission's attempt at better control of state cars was at least partially effective.

When a used article of equipment could be traded in advantageously on its replacement, the department would note that fact on its requisition for the new property and the purchasing division would include an allowance for the trade-in in its purchase order. Ordinarily no attempt was made to ascertain the possibility of transferring the equipment to some other department and utilizing it there.

State institutions and the departments that operated on dedicated funds, such as the Highway Department, usually sold personal property as they pleased, without the supervision and control of the Commission of Administration and Finance. Most other departments were very reluctant to part with any property except on a trade-in, since money received from the sale of such property would go into the state's general revenue fund.[15] Since departments built up a strong proprietary interest in property that came into

[14] Information from files of the Department of Administration and Finance.
[15] *Mason's Minnesota Statutes,* 1927, Sec. 58–1.

their possession, they were reluctant to dispose of any property, whether it was in use or not, unless they received value in return.

Public Reporting

Although the function of public reporting did not receive particular attention when the reorganization act was passed, the Department of Administration and Finance probably had more responsibilities connected with this function than any other state official or department. The commission, however, made no regular public reports of its own, its only regular publication being the biennial budget document.

Most important power of the department in this respect was the authority that the printing law gave to the state printer "to edit and condense reports" that state departments and agencies had prepared for printing.[16] Neither the state printer nor the commission ran the risk of incurring official displeasure by attempting to use this power. In 1926 the report of one elective official was delayed for a few weeks, and it seemed that the commission might make some editorial changes in it, but it was eventually printed as submitted.

There was very little administrative restriction on departments desiring to print reports. The statutes on printing provided that the reports of certain named departments and officials, together with such items as were designated "executive documents," should be printed regularly and were to be paid from a general printing and binding appropriation that was made to the commission.[17] This had the effect of preventing numerous departments from printing their reports. After the first budget commissioner had recommended the discontinuance of the general printing and binding appropriation, the legislature stopped making new appropriations for the purpose,[18] and thereafter the expense of printing reports was usually charged to the appropriations of the respective departments. There is no record that the commission prevented any reports from being printed at department expense after that time.

[16] *Ibid.*, Sec. 5674. He also could "decline to publish such portions as he shall decide may be omitted without injury to the state."

[17] *Ibid.* The attorney general ruled on August 5, 1926, that publication of reports not named in *Session Laws*, 1925, Ch. 359, was permitted under the class of "executive documents," provided the governor directed such publication and distribution as a matter of public interest.

[18] In 1927. The balance of the old appropriation was carried forward and used for some printing for several years afterwards, however.

Printing the *Legislative Manual* was also a responsibility of the Big Three after 1931. Most of its material, pertaining to such things as election returns, official lists of newspapers, and lists of county officers, was prepared by the secretary of state, but the Department of Administration and Finance bore the responsibility for preparing some of the material on state government, for deciding the format, and for supervising the printing. The first commission made some changes in the form of the book in the interests of economy, but no attempt was ever made to make general changes in the content. The book was never envisioned as a general public report on state government.

One provision of the reorganization act with respect to public reporting was a mandate that "the Comptroller at all times shall have free access to the books, records, accounts, and papers of the several departments, and shall verify all accounting statements included in department records before the publication thereof" (Article III, Section 10). This authority was not used. Neither the financial statements in the reports of operating departments nor the reports of the state auditor and state treasurer ever carried a certification of the comptroller as to their correctness, and on some occasions at least the reports appeared before an audit was made of the accounts summarized in the reports.

The lack of public reports on the state's financial affairs as a whole, except for a brief annual report of the treasurer and the biennial report of the auditor, has always characterized Minnesota's financial administration. The reorganization act of 1925 contemplated the possibility of making periodical reports on the state's business available to the public, but nothing ever came of the following provision:

The Comptroller shall prepare and submit to the Commission from time to time as required, a summary statement showing the reports and expenditures of the various departments, the balances standing to the credit of each, and the expense of operation of each for the period covered by such statement, such statement to be in convenient form for publication if the Commission shall so direct. [Article III, Section 10]

The only attempt to make regular reports to the public on the condition of the state's finances was in 1939, when for three successive months [19] the budget commissioner published a small

[19] March 1, April 1, May 1, 1939.

mimeographed booklet setting forth the preceding month's operations by funds, cash balances in the treasury by funds, information on the estimated and actual receipts for the year to date for the general revenue fund, and a forecast of revenue fund operations for the remainder of the year. These booklets were distributed primarily to members of the legislature, to newspapers, and to libraries. Abolition of the commission brought an end to the experiment.

Service to Newspapers

In addition to his duties pertaining to state printing and advertising, the state expert printer was responsible for service to newspapers in the measurement of legal notices. An old statute provided that in the case of a dispute over the price to be paid for any legal notice published in a newspaper, the notice should be submitted to the state printer and he should measure it and determine the correct charges in accordance with the legal rates established by law.[20]

In practice most items were submitted to the printer in advance of any possible dispute; the country newspaper publishers did not attempt to determine the correct charges on some legal notices but sent a copy of the publication to the printer for him to certify the correct charge. Determination of the amount due was more than a matter of measuring the number of lines in the advertisement; consideration had to be given to the size of the type face, and adjustments had to be made for differences in the width of the characters.

This work usually absorbed most of the time of one of the two clerks in the state printer's office. Certain items, such as probate court notices and advertisements of sheriff's sales, were published throughout the year; others, such as county and village financial statements and personal property and delinquent tax lists, were seasonal in character and placed a heavy burden on the printer's office during a few weeks of each year. This type of work bore no relationship to the state printer's other duties in the procurement of printing and advertising for state agencies, but it was a task requiring an impartial referee and the state expert printer apparently was the logical person to do it.

Mailing Station Service

When the erection of a new state office building was authorized in 1929, the legislature passed an act providing for the creation of

[20] *Mason's Minnesota Statutes,* 1927, Sec. 10938.

a central mailing station through which all outgoing mail of departments housed in the capitol buildings would pass.[21] The law provided that departments should pay the postage on their mail through a system of advance deposits, but the absence of an appropriation for operating expenses kept the law from going into effect.

In 1937 the Commission of Administration and Finance made a plea for an appropriation to finance the establishment of such a mailing station,[22] and the legislature agreed to make a small grant for the purpose.[23] A survey of a similar system in another state by an employee of the commission preceded the opening of the central mailing station on July 1, 1937. Departments were requested to turn in loose postage on hand for credit, departments could draw voucher warrants for postage thereafter only to the mailing station (except for field offices and institutions), and meter machines were installed in the mailing station to speed the handling of the mail.

The station operated under the general supervision of the commission, though after it was running smoothly, responsibility for the details of operation were turned over to the custodian of the capitol buildings. All departmental offices housed in the buildings, except those of the secretary of state, whose motor vehicle division business had caused him to install mailing machines of his own some years earlier, came under the plan. The commission exempted the secretary of state of its own volition.

Substantial savings, estimated at several times the cost of operating the station, were reported. These savings were attributed to four causes. First, postage stamps were removed from the hands of more than a hundred state employees and officials, who had previously had the opportunity to use the stamps without supervision.[24] Second, the clerks in the station secured lower postage rates for circulars and other matter mailed by the state departments, which apparently had been unaware of the advantages of using certain permits and bulk mailing rates. Third, the cost of mail from

[21] *Session Laws*, 1929, Ch. 350.
[22] Through the *Sixth Biennial Budget*, 1937–39, p. 97, and through personal requests to the appropriate legislative committees.
[23] *Session Laws*, 1937, Ch. 457, Sec. 17, item 7 ($7,000 for two years).
[24] The majority of the employees were without doubt honest, but capitol employees sometimes remarked on such coincidences as the purchase of additional postage by some departments about the time that private Christmas cards were mailed. The old system also offered opportunities for using state postage for political purposes without detection; under the new system it would be possible to send political matter through the central mailing station, but the meter mark on the envelope would reveal that it had been so mailed.

St. Paul to Minneapolis was reduced by securing a Minneapolis meter machine, by placing a local rate of postage upon letters and packages destined for Minneapolis, and by transporting the mail directly to a Minneapolis postal station.[25] Fourth, there was a release of departmental employees' time, since they were no longer needed to affix stamps to thousands of letters each day; obviously the meter machines in the mailing station were faster than the hand method.

[25] The *Seventh Biennial Budget* (p. 384) reported a saving of $1,937.37 in the first year due to this reason alone.

Chapter 10

CONCLUSIONS

THE establishment of the Minnesota Commission of Administration and Finance in 1925 was heralded by its sponsors and friends as "a new era in state government" and as "a landmark of governmental progress." The opposition denounced it as "false economy" and as "a dangerous concentration of power in the hands of the chief executive." Like most other governmental institutions, the Big Three failed to live up to the expectations of either its proponents or its critics.

Minnesota was among the first of the states whose leaders saw the need for strengthening the position of the governor in relation to administrative departments and agencies, but by the time public opinion, aroused by rapidly mounting taxes and governmental expenditures, was ready to support definite legislative action in this direction, a number of other commonwealths had already acted. In consequence, the Minnesota reorganization act of 1925, the report of the House Interim Committee that proposed it, and the campaign speeches of the gubernatorial candidate advocating it clearly reflected the influence of earlier legislation in other states, notably Massachusetts and Illinois. The Massachusetts Commission on Administration and Finance, established in 1923, unmistakably furnished the pattern for the Minnesota legislation of 1925, though differences may be noted between the two statutes, especially in the provisions for personnel administration. The commission idea appealed to Minnesota and the initial results claimed in Massachusetts were mentioned frequently during the election campaign of 1924 and the legislative debates of 1925. The Illinois administrative code of 1917, with its system of single-headed departments including a Department of Finance, was cited in contrast to the Minnesota proposal as involving an excessive concentration of power, subject to abuse under a weak or corrupt chief executive.

Governmental agencies, as all other human institutions, reflect in some measure the purposes and abilities of those who direct and control them. The 1925 act clearly made the Commission of Administration and Finance an instrument of the governor. Theodore

141

COMMISSION OF ADMINISTRATION AND FINANCE

Christianson, chief executive of the state during the first five and a half years of the commission's existence, had been a determined advocate of the reorganization idea as a leader in the House of Representatives, as a member of the Interim Committee, and as a candidate for governor. His watchword was "economy." His philosophy of government is perhaps nowhere more clearly expressed than in his farewell message to the legislature in January 1931, when he said, "It has been my belief that one of the best ways in which a government can serve the people is to make the burdens it imposes on them as light as possible." Thus the Big Three began its work motivated by the pledge of its chief to halt the mounting expenditures of state government. The extent to which this objective was realized is partially reflected in the following tabulation of revenue fund appropriations from 1915 to 1929 cited in Christianson's farewell message:

1915	$18,019,503.60	1923	40,278,669.88
1917	21,833,263.16	1925	40,329,953.00
1919	32,044,022.26	1927	40,629,834.00
1921	36,711,292.97	1929	42,261,746.25

Furthermore, Governor Christianson was able to report as he left office in 1931 an 80 per cent reduction in state indebtedness payable by the general taxpayer. Certificates of indebtedness had decreased from $15,719,000 to $3,567,758, and he pointed to the possibility of a bondless state in 1933 if the same rate of debt payment was continued. He credited these accomplishments not only to his own use of the item veto power and his resistance to proposals for unnecessary new state activities and increased personnel, but also to the expenditure control and central purchasing functions of the Commission of Administration and Finance.

Naturally, Governor Christianson's successors from 1931 to 1939 — Floyd Olson, Hjalmar Petersen, and Elmer A. Benson — all Farmer-Laborites, all interested primarily in programs of social reform, all confronted by demands for shifting governmental costs from local units to the state and by the urgent necessity of large state expenditures for relief and public assistance, found an institution such as the Big Three, conceived and developed largely as a means of curtailing expenditures, of relatively limited assistance. Its possibilities as a positive instrument for directing and coordinating the increasing number and variety of state administrative agencies and activities had not been explored to any great extent in the formative years, and they continued to be largely ignored in the later years. Centralization of personnel control and patronage constitute perhaps the most notable exception to this statement. Materially expanded and improved in 1932 as a means of strengthening the budget and the processes of expenditure control, this centralization developed to some degree in the direction of an organized personnel system, although, in the absence of civil service legislation, it was used as a means of controlling job placements in the interest of the party in power.

Members of the commission, appointive by the governor and removable by him at any time without cause, were clearly responsible to the chief executive. Though appointed for six-year terms, they actually served at his pleasure, readily submitting resignations whenever he wanted to replace them. In experience and ability, the majority of the commissioners were reasonably well fitted to perform their duties. Personal and political considerations without much reference to other qualifications apparently controlled the choice of some of the members.

Legislative attitude toward the Big Three was never very cordial or cooperative, especially in the Senate. Apparently, many legislators could not or would not become reconciled to a system of budgeting and expenditure control that involved, in part, reliance upon the judgment and expertness of an administrative officer or commission. Except in the case of Theodore Christianson, the governors were not willing to support vigorously the budget recommendations of the Big Three before the legislature, nor did they assume responsibility for approving or modifying those recommendations in advance of legislative consideration. The budget commissioner and other members of the commission were consulted frequently on budget requests by the House Appropriations Committee but not by the Senate Finance Committee, and final legislative appropriations often exceeded budget recommendations. Proposals for further departmental consolidation and for improved procedures of fiscal management were accepted only tardily, if at all, and then for the most part when advocated by incoming governors, without particular reference to commission action.

Appropriations for the work of the commission were always meager and generally inadequate for the effective discharge of its powers and responsibilities. Because of the economy program the first commission was apparently reluctant to request more. Later commissions encountered the hostility of a conservative majority in the upper house or gubernatorial indifference or both. Appreciation of the value of auxiliary services here, as everywhere, proved difficult to obtain. Lacking sufficient funds, the commission was unable to employ a staff adequate in size or skill to scrutinize carefully the budget estimates and allotment requests, to maintain an effective system of budgetary accounts, to purchase commodities and services necessary to meet a variety of departmental needs, to investigate requests for increased staff and salaries, and to postaudit accounts. Such inability to do its jobs thoroughly and well undoubtedly lowered its prestige and strengthened the arguments of its critics.

Central fiscal control agencies inevitably encounter some criticism and occasional open hostility from the heads of spending departments. Consequently it is not surprising that the establishment and functioning of the Commission of Administration and Finance resulted in opposition from the heads of some state agencies, notably the elective officers and members of the Railroad and Warehouse Commission and the university. The latter claimed and won exemption on constitutional grounds. The former were unsuccessful in their efforts to win freedom from control, but they could always be counted upon to voice public criticism of the commission at opportune times and to disparage its efforts whenever chance afforded.

There is very little evidence to substantiate the claim that the commission, through its budget and allotment procedures, seriously hampered the work of the departments. Some differences arose, and undoubtedly errors of judgment were committed, often because an adequate staff was lacking. As one contemporary observer rather extravagantly put it when writing of the 1925 act, "In the making of the budget the commissioner of the budget will need the cube of Solomon's wisdom to know whether he is checking poor departmental policy or is intruding unwisely on good policy." Departmental budget estimates were markedly curtailed, and quarterly allotments were reduced, but there is convincing evidence of the need for such fiscal control.

The commission also demonstrated to some degree that such an agency can achieve economies without resort to its powers of supervision and control. By the processes of inquiry, advice, and negotiation the commission occasionally initiated economy measures and

144

CONCLUSIONS

aided departments in getting the greatest possible return for their money. Unquestionably, however, the strong emphasis upon economy for economy's sake that characterized the commission's work during the early formative years tended to alienate the operating departments and thus militated against the usefulness of the commission as a staff aid in organization, accounting, personnel, procurement, and office management problems.

The dedication by constitution and statute of certain revenues to particular departments or functions and the customary reappropriation of unused balances in departmental appropriations removed, in effect, a very large percentage of the total state expenditures from the budget-making power of the commission.

Failure to develop a budgetary accounting system on an accrual basis militated seriously against an effective control of expenditures. Substantial progress toward the establishment of encumbrance accounting, however, was being made shortly before the commission was abolished. The absence of cooperation between the budget and purchasing commissioners interfered with the effort to enforce quarterly allotments, and repeated appeals by the commission to the departments to keep within their allotments appear not to have received the active assistance of the governors. Lack of a common objective or purpose also had an adverse effect upon the work of the commission in later years. Both the personnel and purchasing divisions were pursuing aims that were not in harmony with the economy objectives of the budget division, in spite of the fact that the personnel and budget divisions were under the same commissioner.

Difficulties between the auditor, with his powers of pre-audit and central proprietary accounting, and the commission, with its powers of allotment control, budgetary accounting, and postauditing, were to be expected. A more logical division of responsibility would have vested authority for budgetary control, accounting, and pre-auditing in the commission, and the postaudit function in the auditor's office. However, the two agencies managed to perform their closely related duties with a minimum of overlapping and friction. Inadequate accounting by funds in the auditor's office hampered the commission, the governor, and the legislature in ascertaining the fiscal condition of the state and in reporting on it to the public.

Placing the postaudit, or public examiner's function, under the

Big Three did furnish the budget division with a corps of examiners reasonably familiar with state agencies in the preparation of the biennial budget, though this perhaps delayed the development of a staff of full-time budget examiners. It also furnished incoming governors with a convenient and responsible agency to investigate the conduct of departments under outgoing administrations. Because the independent elective auditor was responsible for the pre-audit of expenditures, the postaudits of state agencies made by members of the comptroller's staff centered upon an investigation of receipts. Relatively few irregularities were found. In general, the performance of the postaudit function showed a steady improvement during the commission's history.

The procurement and personnel functions of the Big Three gave rise, perhaps, to the most criticism. Limited in its authority over particular departments, concentrating largely upon the technical task of buying, and, especially in later years, following questionable methods of soliciting bids and awarding contracts, the purchasing division hardly made an enviable record for itself, though the estimated savings it achieved in the purchase of sizable quantities of particular commodities were often cited as one of the more tangible accomplishments of the reorganization act. Dissatisfaction with the procurement of printing after 1931 was evident both within and without the commission. Actual selection of the state printer by the governor rather than by the commission appears to have been responsible in some measure for this unfavorable situation.

Efforts in 1927 and 1934 to provide an adequate classification and compensation plan for state employees, and the initiation of a pay-roll certification system in 1931–32 — both important and valuable elements in a public personnel system — were overshadowed in terms of legislative inquiry and public discussion by the use of the personnel division of the Big Three as a central employment and patronage office. Changes in party control in 1931 and in 1939 and widespread unemployment in the intervening years intensified the pressure for jobs. The resultant consequences to the state service and to the party in power hastened the enactment of a state civil service law in 1939.

Relatively little was gained, except perhaps in the first years of the Department of Administration and Finance, through the use of the three-member commission form of organization. Even from 1925 to 1931 Comptroller Rines, who was chairman of the commission, seems to have served in substantial degree as the head of the department, with the budget and purchasing commissioners as his chief subordinates. Admittedly, however, the first commissioners met together frequently, discussed major policies, and functioned as a group in budget investigations and hearings. In later years each commissioner assumed, to a very marked degree, the responsibility for his particular statutory duties and the commission as a whole met only to ratify their individual decisions and actions. On several occasions members of the commission refused to accept responsibility for the decisions of their colleagues, pleading ignorance or the pressure of their own particular work. On the contrary, instances did occur in which one or two commissioners successfully protested against what they considered the unwise action of another commissioner.

It may be that the basic difference between the earlier and later periods is that Governor Christianson, keenly interested in the success of the experiment and given the opportunity to select all the members of the commission at one time, was successful in finding a group of men who could work together. The leadership of one member of this group has been noted. Observing the entire record, however, it is not difficult to find evidence to support the action taken in 1939 in substituting for the commission a single-headed Department of Administration, with principal assistants in charge of budgeting, purchasing, printing, and public property, and in reestablishing a separate Department of the Public Examiner.

The Minnesota Commission of Administration and Finance did not accomplish all that its sponsors had promised. In its partial successes and frequent failures, however, it demonstrated the basic soundness of the theory of central fiscal control through an agency responsible to and functioning on behalf of the chief executive. It accustomed legislators and operating departments to centralized budgetary, procurement, and personnel methods and processes, thus paving the way for subsequent legislative action and administrative improvements. Finally, it demonstrated that effective organization, competent personnel, a state service based upon merit, and an actively interested and administration-conscious governor are essential to the successful application of the theory which lay back of its creation.

BIBLIOGRAPHY

Books and Articles

AKRE, EDNA H. "The League of Women Voters: Its Organization and Work," an unpublished thesis in the University of Minnesota Library, 1926.

An Analysis of Minnesota State Fiscal Operations, 1932–1940. Minnesota Institute of Governmental Research Bulletin No. 11. March 1941.

BUCK, A. E. *The Reorganization of State Governments in the United States.* New York, 1938.

CHRISTIANSON, THEODORE. *Minnesota: A History of the State and Its People.* 5 vols. Chicago, 1935.

COOKE, G. W. "The Evolution of the Minnesota Budget System," an unpublished thesis in the University of Minnesota Library, 1925.

JOHNSON, VIOLET. "A Survey of the Administration of the State Government in Minnesota," an unpublished thesis in the University of Minnesota Library, 1929.

LAMBIE, M. B. *An Approach to Problems of Administration in the State of Minnesota.* League of Minnesota Municipalities Bulletin No. 3. Minneapolis, 1924.

LEAGUE OF MINNESOTA MUNICIPALITIES. *Legislative Bulletin No. 4.* March 1925.

"Minnesota Tax Conference Resolutions," *Minnesota Municipalities*, 9:18–19 (February 1924).

Minnesota Woman Voter (monthly publication of the Minnesota League of Women Voters), especially for 1924 and 1925.

RINES, HENRY. "The Department of Administration and Finance," *Minnesota Municipalities*, 13:517–19 (November 1928).

THURSTON, JOHN H. "Personnel Administration in the State Government of Minnesota," an unpublished thesis in the University of Minnesota Library, 1932.

WITTICH, MRS. F. W. "How Minnesota Reorganized Her State Administration," *California Tax Digest*, 2:7–13 (January 1926).

YOUNG, J. S. "Reorganization of the Administrative Branch of the Minnesota Government," *American Political Science Review*, 20:69–76 (February 1926).

———. "Reorganization of the Administrative Branch of the Minnesota Government," *Minnesota Law Review*, 10:40–47 (December 1925).

Reports, Documents, Laws, and Other Official Sources

Biennial Budget Documents, 1927–39.

Biennial Budget Summaries of Appropriations, 1927–39.

Blank forms and letters, memoranda, manuals of instruction, and special reports, issued by the Commission of Administration and Finance (in the files of the Minnesota Department of Administration).

Budget Recommendations of Governor Harold E. Stassen to the 51st Regular Session of the Minnesota State Legislature, February 1, 1939.

Classes, Grades, and Titles of State Employes, with Class Specifications, as determined by the Commission of Administration and Finance, Division of Personnel, January 1935.

Election campaign documents, 1925–39 (in the Minnesota Historical Society).

BIBLIOGRAPHY

Estimates of Appropriations Required for the biennial period ending July 31, 1919. Also the corresponding estimates for 1921, 1923, and 1925.

Final Report of the Efficiency and Economy Commission, 1914.

FITERMAN, HARRY. "Report of the Minnesota State Finance and Tax Survey," *St. Paul Dispatch,* November 18, 1937, and subsequent issues.

Fourth Biennial Report of the Minnesota Tax Commission, 1914, pp. 154–75.

LEAGUE OF MINNESOTA MUNICIPALITIES, *Minnesota Year Book,* 1934, pp. 39–122.

Mason's Minnesota Statutes, (2 vols., St. Paul, 1927; supplement, 1940).

Messages of the Governors of Minnesota, 1925–39.

Minnesota Legislative Manual, 1925–39.

"Minutes of the Commission of Administration and Finance," Books A, B, C, and D, 1927–39.

Opinions of the Attorney General, 1925–39.

"Personnel Survey of the State of Minnesota," made by the Commission of Administration and Finance, July 1, 1928.

Preliminary Report of the Efficiency and Economy Commission, 1914.

Reorganization of State Government, Report of Interim Committee to House of Representatives, 1925.

Report from the Joint Senate and House Investigating Committee Covering the Acts and Activities of the Various Governmental Departments and Agencies of the State of Minnesota, 1939 Legislative Session and 1939–40 Interim.

Report of Investigating Committee of the Senate Created Under Resolution No. 2, For the Purpose of Investigating All Departments of the State Government of Minnesota: Individual Report of Senator Richard N. Gardner, 1935.

Report of Investigating Committee of the Senate created under Resolution No. 2, For the Purpose of Investigating All Departments of the State Government of Minnesota: James A. Carley, Chairman, 1935.

Report of the examination by Hines and Bachman, Certified Public Accountants, January 16, 1928 (typewritten copy in the files of the Minnesota Department of Administration).

Report of the Legislative Tax Commission of Investigation and Inquiry, 1937.

Salary Scales for State Employes, as classified by the Commission of Administration and Finance, Division of Personnel, January 1935.

Salary Scales for State Employes. Proposed by the Commission of Administration and Finance, Division of Personnel, and Recommended in the Biennial Budget, 1935–37, January 1935.

Session Laws of the State of Minnesota, 1925–39.

Newspapers

Files of the following newspapers, 1925–39: *Askov American, Dawson Sentinel, Fairmont Daily Sentinel, Fergus Falls Journal, Mid-West American, Minneapolis Journal, Minneapolis Tribune, Minnesota Leader, Minnesota Union Advocate, Red Wing Republican, St. Paul Daily News, St. Paul Dispatch, St. Paul Pioneer Press,* and *Willmar Daily Tribune.*

Cases

State ex rel. Thomas Yapp *et al.* v. Ray P. Chase *et al.* 165 Minn. 268 (1925).

State ex rel. University of Minnesota *et al.* v. Ray P. Chase, 175 Minn. 259 (1928).

COMMISSION OF ADMINISTRATION AND FINANCE

State ex rel. J. J. Mergens *et al.* v. Charles M. Babcock *et al.*, 175 Minn. 583 (1928).
State ex rel. Charles Weaver v. Charles M. Babcock, 175 Minn. 590 (1928).
Edward Fanning *et al.* v. University of Minnesota *et al.*, 183 Minn. 222 (1931).
State ex rel. William H. Kinler v. Henry Rines, 185 Minn. 49 (1931).
John J. Regan *et al.* v. Charles M. Babcock *et al.*, 188 Minn. 192 (1933).
State ex rel. Harry H. Peterson v. Ray Quinlivan, 198 Minn. 65 (1936).

INDEX

Accounting, revision recommended, 24; records installed in state auditor's office discarded, 24; inadequacy criticized, 42–43; accrual system, 43, 83n; transfer suggested, 43, 48; legal and practical aspects summarized, 90; types distinguished, 90; for disbursements, 92; central system criticized, 98; division of responsibilities criticized, 145

Accounting, budgetary: needed, 81; departmental forms, 82; changed, 83; duty of Big Three, 92; lack of accrual system, 145

Accounting, departmental: supervision, 92, 98–99; uniform system never formulated, 99

Accounting, local, 99

Administration, Commissioner of, *see* Commissioner of Administration

Advertising, state: economies, 86; supervision by state printer, 115

Agencies, state, number, 2

Agricultural societies, expenditures not subject to allotment control, 81

Agricultural Society, State, after reorganization act, 109n

Agriculture, consolidation of activities recommended, 70

Agriculture, Commissioner of, appointed Commissioner of Dairy and Food, 131

Agriculture, Department of, food inspections for, 131; consolidation with Department of Dairy and Food, 131

Akre, Edna H., cited, 9n

Allotments, quarterly: first required, 20; of University of Minnesota refused approval, 25; failure to use as positive factor, 42; procedure, 77–81; not used to balance revenue fund operations, 78n; amendments, 79–80; conflicts, 80; enforcement through accounts, 81; payments in excess, 82; supplemental, approved, 82–83; expenditures charged in quarter in which bills incurred, 83; policy explained by Governor Christianson, 87–88; exceeded in purchases for departments, 108. *See also* Expenditure control

Appropriations, for Big Three, 59–62; ledger, 82

Appropriations, continuing: criticized, 42; effect on budget making, 68, 145

Appropriations, deficiency, record *1928–39*, 83

Architectural service, provisions, 109–10

Attorney General, intervention in suits against Big Three, 31; dispute with Big Three, 35, 112; investigation of Farmer-Labor administration, 47

Attorney General, opinions: favorable to Big Three, 33–34; unfavorable, 34–36; influences upon, 36; exempting relief expenditures and rural credit payments from allotment control, 81; questioning constitutionality of comptroller's review of auditor's actions, 94n; upholding comptroller's authority to prescribe accounting records in treasurer's and auditor's offices, 99n; concerning advertising for bids, 107–8

Audit, Board of: postaudit of treasurer's office transferred to comptroller, 91n, 94; quarterly audits of treasurer's office, 95

Auditing, types, 90; legal and practical aspects summarized, 90; division of responsibilities questioned, 145. *See also* Current audit; Postaudit; Pre-audit

Auditor, State: machine accounting records discarded, 24, 98; accounts prescribed by comptroller, 33; duties in enforcing expenditure control, 77; responsibility for legal pre-audit, 91, 92–93; duty to maintain central accounts, 91–92; purpose of accounts, 92; appropriation ledger, 92n; records postaudited by comptroller, 95; independent audit of accounts, 97–98; change in central accounting records recommended, 98

Audits, special: of auditor's and treasurer's offices, 24, 97–98; of state offices and departments, *1939*, 46–47

Austin, Herbert W., appointed purchasing commissioner, 19; assistant discharged, 32; personal history, 52

Automobiles, state-owned, use controlled, 86, 134–35

Axness, C. E., table on appropriations, 74

Bemidji Teachers' College, building project: bid procedure questioned, 35; investigation by architects' association, 44; report, 93n

151

28; opposition to increased educational appropriations, 29; *1930* campaign for United States Senate, 29; participation in budgeting, 70, 71; use of item veto, 72; attitude on economy, 87–88; recommendation for consolidation of departments, 132n; use of Commission for reorganization studies, 133; accomplishments through Commission, 141–42

Civil Service, Department of: recommended by budget commissioner, 40; created, 49

Civil service, recommended by Governor Hjalmar Petersen, 39. *See also* Merit system

Civil Service Commission, recommendations for, 126

Classification of positions, lack cited in Interim Committee report, 11; Commission plan in *1927*, 25; powers of Big Three, 33–34; *1935* plan suspended, 38; *1927* plan, 117–19; *1935* plan, 119–21

Commission of Administration and Finance, influences on history of, 1; proposed, 12; composition, 12; authority, 12; history characterized, 19; first appointments, 19; early problems, 19–20; early disputes, 20–22; early accomplishments, 22; tested in *1926* campaign, 22; constitutionality of expenditure control over university tested, 25–27; powers to approve highway contracts upheld, 27; controversy with university over budget requests, 28–29; relation to State Office Building Commission, 29; appointments by Governor Floyd Olson, 30; difficulties with elective officials, 31; criticized on highway contracts, 32; internal difficulties during Olson administration, 32–33; adverse opinions of attorney general, 34–35; investigation by Senate committee, 37, 38; appropriation reduced, 38; reorganization proposed, 43; target in *1938* campaign, 45; abolition advocated, 45; changes in personnel in *1939*, 46; investigation, 47; abolished, 49; organization, 50, 55–58; comptrollers, 50–51; personnel, 50–53; budget commissioners, 51–52; purchasing commissioners, 52–53; meetings, 53–55; minutes, 54; organization chart, 56; executive secretary, 58–59; appropriations and expenditures, 59–62; staff, 62; powers in budget making, 63; expenditure control, 76; quarterly allotment forms issued, 77; approval of allotments, 78–79; publicity on allotment request cuts, 79n; weakness in

expenditure control system, 82; efforts to enforce allotments, 82; deficiency appropriation record, 83; pre-audit power, 84–85, 90; relation to governor in expenditure control, 87–89; authority to examine all financial transactions, 91; duty to keep allotment and encumbrance accounts, 92; purpose of accounts, 92; power to supervise departmental accounts, 92; appropriation ledger, 92n; pre-audit, 93; postaudit of accounts, 96; central purchasing, 102–4; beginning of purchasing work, 104–5; given supervision of central storeroom, 108; responsibility for building contracts, 109–10; procurement of architectural and engineering services, 109–10; review of highway contracts, 111, 111n; authority concerning rentals of buildings and equipment, 111–12; responsibility for utilities service, 112; authority with respect to bonds for state officials, 112, 112n; control of state printing, 113–14; experiences in personnel administration, 116; personnel powers, 116–17; cited, 119n, 120n; duty to secure information about new state employees, 121; control over departments through pay-roll checking, 122; salary reductions enforced, 122–23; limited powers concerning recruitment and removal, 123–26; effect of recruitment and removal functions, 126; responsibilities for employee relations, 127–29; order on political activities of state employees, 127; policies concerning state employee unions, 128; studies and surveys of administration, 130, 131; recommendations for reorganization, 132, 133–34; responsibility for public reporting, 136–38; recommendation for central mailing station, 139; effect on state expenditures, 142; relationship to governors, 141, 142–43; appropriations for, 143–44; relation to departments, 144; accomplishments and failures, 144–47

Commissioner of Administration, office recommended, 43; office created, 49

Compensation, plan of *1927* not effective after *1930*, 119; plan of *1935*, 119–20; plan of *1935* nullified by appropriation act, 120–21. *See also* Salary schedules; Salaries

Comptroller, friction with chief public examiner, 32; authority to prescribe accounts in auditor's and treasurer's offices, 33; duties in enforcing allotment control, 77; right to review actions of

INDEX

for, 85–87; supported by governors, 87–89; attitude of departments, 144. *See also* Allotments

Farmer-Labor party, in *1928* campaign, 28; in *1930* election, 30; charges by Senate investigating committee, 38; *1936* victories, 40; administrations investigated, 47; patronage activities, 125
Finance, Department of, recommended, 3, 43; plan omitted, 4
Finance and Taxation, Department of, recommended, 45
Financial administration, changes recommended in budgets, 69–70
Fiterman, Harry, report on Minnesota Finance and Tax Survey, 41–42
Furlow, Allen J., vote on reorganization bill opposed, 15n

Game and Fish, Department of, authority of Big Three questioned, 24; contracts subject to Big Three, 34. *See also* Conservation, Department of
Gislason, J. B., service on House Interim Committee, 8
Golling, Richard, executive secretary of Commission, 59
Gordon, S. Y., service as state printer, 114n
Governor, participation in budget processes, 63–64, 68, 70, 71, 72; recommendations for borrowing, 69; nonattendance at budget hearings, 70–71; budget messages, 71; veto powers, 72; expenditure control, 87–89; approval of expenditures in excess of allotments, 88; influence over postaudits, 100–1; regulation of conditions of state employment, 128; power to appoint one person to two positions, 131–32; relation to Big Three, 141–43. *See also* names of individual governors
Gravlin, Leslie M., appointed commissioner of administration, 49

Hammond, Winfield S., Governor: approval of report of Efficiency and Economy Commission, 4; legislative opposition, 5n
Hayes, George, appointed assistant director of personnel, 117
Health, Department of, food inspection for departments of Agriculture and Dairy and Food, 131
Highways, Department of, contracts subject to approval of Big Three, 27; suits on contracts, 31–32; purchases held exempt from bid requirements, 36; political obligations of employees, 36, 127; payment of Big Three employees, 62; not summoned for budget hearings, 65; purchase orders not submitted for pre-audit, 85; purchasing staff kept separate from Commission, 104; purchasing staff assigned to Commission office, 105, 105n; testing laboratory, 106n; responsibility for contract procedure, 110–11; rental of equipment, 112; use of personnel classification plan, 121; personnel director appointed, 125; opposition to control over motor vehicles, 135. *See also* Contracts
Hines and Bachmann, report on auditor's and treasurer's offices, 24n, 97–98
Hitchcock, R. W., advocate of abolition of Commission, 32
Hotel Inspection, Division of, employees subject to Commission, 123
House of Representatives, Public Buildings Committee's recommendation concerning state office building, 29; Appropriations Committee, 73; purchases by Big Three, 105

Illinois Department of Finance, rejected as model for Minnesota, 141
Indebtedness, estimates not contained in all budgets, 69
Interim Committee: on State Reorganization, proposed in *1911* and *1913*, 3; on Civil Administration, *1915*, 7–8; on Administrative Reorganization, creation opposed by Senate in *1921*, 8; on Administrative Reorganization, House of Representatives, *1923*, 8–13
Interim Tax Committee, recommendations concerning financial administration, 41–43; report cited, 68n
Investigating Committee: Senate, *1935*, report cited, 107n, 112n, 120n; Joint, *1939*, report cited, 47n, 112n

Jerome, Ralph, appointed budget commissioner and personnel director, 46; personal history, 52
Johnson, Joseph, indicted as employment officer, 47
Johnson, Magnus, attack on Big Three, 22
Johnson, Violet, cited, 118n
Judges, district court, expenditures not subject to allotment control, 81

King, Stafford, State Auditor, clash with comptroller, 31

COMMISSION OF ADMINISTRATION AND FINANCE